Rowan Hisayo Buchanan is the author of *Harmless Like You*, *Starling Days* and *The Sleep* ~~Watcher~~  anthologies *Go Home!* and Authors' Club First Novel Aw been shortlisted for the Costa a *New York Times* Editors' Rowan is a fellow of the Ro the recipient of fellowships the Asian American Writers and Kundiman. Her writing has appeared in *Granta*, the *Paris Review* and the *Atlantic* among other places.

~

THE SLEEP WATCHER

Rowan Hisayo Buchanan

sceptre

First published in Great Britain in 2023 by Sceptre
An imprint of Hodder & Stoughton Limited
An Hachette UK company

This paperback edition published in 2024

1

A CIP catalogue record for this title is available from the British Library

Paperback ISBN 9781399710664
ebook ISBN 9781399710640

Typeset in Sabon MT by Hewer Text UK Ltd, Edinburgh
Printed and bound in Great Britain by Clays Ltd, Elcograf S.p.A.

Hodder & Stoughton policy is to use papers that are natural, renewable
and recyclable products and made from wood grown in sustainable
forests. The logging and manufacturing processes are expected to
conform to the environmental regulations of the country of origin.

Hodder & Stoughton Limited
Carmelite House
50 Victoria Embankment
London EC4Y 0DZ

www.sceptrebooks.co.uk

To my favourite demons

'Declare to the Watchers of the heaven who have left the high heaven, the holy eternal place, and have defiled themselves with women, and have done as the children of earth do, and have taken unto themselves wives: "Ye have wrought great destruction on the earth: And ye shall have no peace nor forgiveness of sin: and inasmuch as they delight themselves in their children, the murder of their beloved ones shall they see, and over the destruction of their children shall they lament, and shall make supplication unto eternity, but mercy and peace shall ye not attain."'

– *The Book of Enoch,*
translated R. H. Charles

1

I have never returned to the town. I rarely say its name, only that I grew up a few hours from London. I left before I turned seventeen.

All along the coast there are gate towns – Ramsgate, Margate, Sandgate, Westgate-on-Sea. These are openings in the high, hard cliffs of this island, gates to the water or to the land, depending on your perspective. Then there are the raised headlands – Beachy Head, Minehead, Portishead. These offer the gift of sight.

Our town was neither a head nor a gate. It was a ripple. The town bent towards the sea before rising up again cliffwards. Our cliffs were not famous, and their sides were lumpy and jagged. Tide markers raised their bald heads along our streets. There were three churches, one of which had been converted into a cafe. The local paper bemoaned arsons by suspected youths, but otherwise crime was low.

The sea is now a train ride away but sometimes I see a gull making its white-bellied way through the air to pilfer from our bins or perform some other bastard behaviour. Yesterday I saw two, one swooping after the other in brutality or romance. I told myself I would tell you what happened in that town.

I started wrong. Do you remember? It was while we were making dinner at your flat. Your knife shuttled

3

through the onion. You were blinking back acid tears. Maybe I felt braver because you weren't looking at me. I mentioned the town and added almost casually, *Do you know, while I was living there I stopped dreaming?*

Who can blame you for the reply? *Other people's dreams are always boring.* I didn't argue that this was not a dream but an absence. Instead, I gathered onion peel, swiping the husk into my hand.

I have to try again. It wouldn't be fair to wind myself around your life before I tell you what happened in that place. It's not a thing I have perspective on, even twelve years later. The memories are salty and humid. Perhaps you'll say I was barely out of childhood and that my mistakes were understandable. I hope that afterwards you will still want to pack your stuff, for me to box mine, and for us to conjoin our lives. Or maybe you'll never be able to knot your fingers around mine. Because when you see my hands, you'll remember the damage they've done. You'll decide I'm not the sort of person you want to live with after all.

While you have no time for dreams, you've always had time for books. Whenever I borrow one from your shelves, I trace the graphite underlinings and marvel at your careful attention and the luck of your students. So I thought I'd try to write you one. Or something like one anyway. An account with a beginning, a middle, an end.

Perhaps not everything is quite accurate. There is no one I can check with. I am almost sure that I have not made anyone kinder or crueller than they were. Although it was long ago, I remember that year more clearly than I do last month.

The Facts

That summer, my mind separated from my body as completely as an egg cracked from its shell. The splitting began in those hazy days just after exams were done when everything should have been easy.

Wait.

I've always avoided the subject of childhood or given you generic answers. I owe you the facts.

I had two parents – M and F. The woman who birthed, bottled, and raised me was never Mum or Mummy. She was M. Shortened from *Mem*, the sound my baby lips supposedly made when looking into the moon of her face. My father was named by default. F, said like *Eff*. Kit and Caterpillar, the names they called me, were not on my birth certificate. We lived under pseudonyms. Leo, my brother, was the only one who kept his true name.

F found it easier to sing than to speak. On the weekend, he was in an indie rock band that played local venues and sometimes weddings. Weekdays, he stitched together freelance programming work. He was good with computers but not with business. There was often a skim of stubble along his jaw. He wore thick black jeans and jumpers in colours like mustard and mint. He cut his hair himself, in our sink, and you could tell. His curls were the pale brown seen on men who were once angel-blonde boys. Indeed, his mother had named him after such an angel. Though he didn't look like one anymore, he could name all the angels in the Bible and most of the apocrypha. Music and angels were his great loves. He would have said they were the same thing – a purity missing from most of human life.

M stood very straight and so appeared taller than she was. She worked as a therapist specialising in the problems of teenagers. I sometimes wondered if she'd worked with anyone I knew. Her office was in a larger town about six miles away. A screen on her laptop blocked peeping from the sides. The one time she had revealed a client detail was when she explained why she had stopped working with adults – *He was stressed because he realised his wife and lover had their periods in the same week. He was frightened they'd synchronised, like they both knew something he didn't. That's when I realised adults weren't for me.* She dressed in the colours of the sea – blues, greys, shady greens – as if trying to become part of the local landscape. Although strangers still asked, *But where are you from?* My grandmother was from Japan and something of that distance showed in M's face.

The thing about parents is they're both deadly dull and your first maps of how to live. Mine were no different.

We lived in a terraced house that was part of a line of houses that snaked away from the sea. We'd moved there five years before, when I was eleven, from a larger town inland. At sixteen, I was neither a local nor a stranger. I had friends at school but only one I trusted – Andrew. When he wasn't around, I joined in the games all the girls played. Men watched us that year, on the pier, on the street, in the shops, wherever we went. We sucked orange Calippos by the bus stop, licking the fluorescent juice off our fingers, looking straight into the eyes of pitiful adults with hair growing out of their ears.

I had decided I would lose my virginity to Andrew because he had long-fingered hands – almost but not quite like a girl's – which held even the most gnawed pencil with grace. Also because he was my closest friend. I hadn't told him this decision. I was enjoying having a plan.

Losing my dreams was not a milestone marked in the book M bought about *Your Body's Natural Changes*. Still, it happened.

A Specimen of Night

For a while my dreams had been terrible. They shook my body, shoved the blankets off the bed, and sometimes even knocked me to the floor.

I'll describe the last dream-wracked night I remember. I woke up yet again on the floor. It was old, Victorian probably, pine-yellow and knotted with eyes. My friends had wall-to-wall carpets but Leo had asthma and so we lived with the bare boards. I didn't mind.

Above me, I could see my brother's body lumped in his bed, undisturbed by my crash. I touched my thigh, prodding in search of pain. I wanted to know if I would bruise. I had a generalised interest in my body. There were the obvious widely celebrated transformations of female adolescence, but I was interested in detail. My bones were thickening. Even my hair was shifting in texture. Supposedly, my prefrontal cortex was sprouting new fronds.

Leo sighed in his sleep and his leg twitched. My phone told me it was 1 a.m., but light came from the open door. Looking up, I could see the ceiling pressing in on us. Andrew and I had painted eyes above my bed in black ink, a bit like this –

Though of course not exactly. It is impossible to be exact about the past. Still, I want to use every tool.

F told us that the angels used to be covered in eyes. It amused us to think of them, polka-dotted with vision. So we turned the room into an angel. M had been annoyed but F had approved.

From downstairs came the hum of F's record player, an object which had passed out of retro-coolness a few years before. It played at the lowest turn of the knob – a musical muttering. We usually left the doors in our house open because Leo was scared of the dark and because F was absent-minded, prone to wandering from room to room leaving doors gaping behind him. Noise travelled easily through the house. I went down following the sound – pleased that someone else was awake. Pleased too that it was F.

Leo belonged to M and I belonged to F. Leo was M's the way her hands belonged to her. He was the miracle child, born seven years after me, despite preventative measures.

Not expected but wanted was what M used to say. She held him closer, and she looked at him as if he might not be quite real. I pitied him. It seemed too much to live up to.

F had picked up all the parts of me that M no longer had time to see. When she gave Leo a bath, he read to me. When Leo wouldn't stop crying, F taught me to sing. It wasn't so bad. Leo and I had one bed each, one placemat each, one parent each. And mine was awake and downstairs, waiting for me. So down I went, for water and a break from the dreams which I could still see hanging spiderweb-like in the corner of my vision.

F sat on a kitchen chair, wearing an old band shirt, long boxer shorts and the orange fuzzy dressing gown that was, according to M, The-Most-Hideous-Thing. His eyes were closed in musical-focus. He nodded as I stepped into the kitchen, acknowledging me without opening his eyes. A drink sat on the table in the good glass. We got the good glass at a jumble sale and it sliced the kitchen light into diamonds. I took a less good glass from the cupboard, one that had been fogged by many baptisms through the dishwasher.

I poured myself water. He opened his eyes.

Couldn't sleep, I said.

This was calculated for sympathy because F barely slept at night. He was always moving about the house like a familiar ghost. When not listening to records, F played his own songs about angels who had fallen one by one. He was, if not lapsed, estranged from his God. He seemed forever trying to write some sort of treaty between himself and the great invisible thing he sung to. I was grateful that he didn't play his God-songs in public. The loud boys at school would have sniggered at his unvarnished longing.

He told me that the record we were listening to was written by a guitarist for his dead son. I thought of Leo's breath stopping. His body falling still. I thought of the miracle unspooling and drank my water.

Come sit on my lap, Caterpillar. F pulled his dressing gown over his knees to make a hammock. You might find this strange. I certainly never told anyone at school about it. But I sat and it wasn't the way you might be thinking. It was a ritual that we'd never ended. I don't suppose I knew how. When do you tell your father that you are too big to be held? My toes hung above the floor and I rocked them back and forth in time to the music. And not that I would have admitted it, but it felt good. I let myself lean against him. F smelt of laundry and the oil from his bicycle.

You know I'd die for my family.

You won't have to, I said, *IT workers don't have a high death rate.*

But I would.

I felt the rise and fall of his arm each time he lifted the glass, which was not often. He drank slowly and carefully. He offered me a sip. It tasted of chestnuts mixed with the sharp ethanol smell of the school laboratory. My friends brought orange juice and vodka to school in their reusable water bottles. I was careful not to exhibit too much ease or let my knowledge of that show.

He asked about my subjects at school and whether I knew what I wanted to do afterwards.

I was good at school but didn't love doing anything then. I was an observer, not an actor. I noted the shadow puppets Andrew's hands cast as he drew. And the way F's temples smoothed when he talked about Satan, the angels and saints – all flying or falling creatures. The girls who practised dance routines behind the school, their feet moving in perfect time. The way the sun caught the tips of the tourists' noses. But being a watcher was not an examinable subject and I wouldn't, now, give myself an A – I missed so much.

Find what you love. Practical can come later. No one can avoid practical, he said.

I forget what we talked about next but eventually he said, *Started writing a new song for Sun Songs. Want to hear?*

Every summer in the swelter of August, the local bands went down to the beach to play. The council knew about it and they'd leave a police car dawdling in case things got rowdy. The town liked to say we sang to serenade the turning of the seasons because of our Viking heritage. We'd been stormed long ago by men who worshipped a god of thunder, a god of wisdom, a god of trickery. The festival had actually been started by a few Victorian pre-hippies who styled themselves as druids. It grew into an excuse to listen to music, drink beer, dance on the sand, and run into the sea in your best party dress.

Okay, I said, and slid off his lap to lift the needle from the record.

F hummed low and soft. The sound had a sway. Sometimes his fingers fluttered over his chest as if to say, the guitar part will come in here. The sound was lofty and hopeful. I thought of honey, the dark amber kind flecked with wax that they sold at the bakery. F worked out his songs as sounds before words.

Will you sing it with me? he asked. *It's a duet, I think.*

You know I don't sing.

You used to.

Singing had stopped making sense to me around the time my breasts came in and my armpits grew whiskers. I had stopped wanting everyone to know what was in my heart.

Yeah, because I was six and didn't know I sounded like a frog.

It'll make M really happy.

I wasn't sure this was true. People do that. They say they want you to do something for someone else when they don't want to ask for themselves.

I told you I don't sing.

Okay, Caterpillar. He held up his hands as if I was wielding a gun. But I always felt it when he was upset. The world's mood music shifted.

John Cage composed a silence called 4'33". I saw it a few years before we met. The orchestra sat perfectly still but it was not silent. There was breathing. A cough somewhere. A sense of my own size and noise. Time went slow. That is how I felt when F was upset – a tenseness in my chest as I waited for the concert to continue.

I love you, I said.

I know. And there was more breath in the room.

The Day Before It Happened

My school would break up in a few weeks, at the end of June. But we were all done with GCSEs and none of the teachers seemed concerned with doing more than showing us *educational* videos and letting us nap. I wasn't worried about my results. The shape of standard tests fitted my brain, though M was always telling me not to be so complacent.

Our last class of the day was history and the teacher had put on the *Blackadder* episode about rotten boroughs. I half-watched the on-screen caper and half-watched Andrew, sitting next to me, making a paper boat. It bobbed up and down on his knee. All over his arms were blue biro marks, like one of those Celts from Leo's textbook. I pictured Andrew running down a hill screaming, his stringy arms flailing. And then I thought what it might be like to be so close to him that biro came off on my skin in blue clouds. Forgive me for sharing this, I know you aren't the jealous type and I was so young. Nothing I wanted then was elegant or beautiful. It was awkward and hungry, and I knew it. Which is why I was waiting for the right moment.

I lifted the boat from his knee and placed it carefully on the crown of my head, keeping my back as straight as the stiff plastic chair. It was so light that I couldn't feel it. I had to keep reaching my hand up to check it was there.

After school, everyone was going to get pizza and talk shit about the teachers and each other. It was easy to imagine how the evening would go. I'd nod along, that I too thought that the swimming teacher was a creep, that his eyes lingered on our bodies in their green Lycra. When they wore out the gossip, my classmates would end up mouth-to-mouth with someone they would have to decide they either loved or despised the next day.

But I headed home, because *there was dinner waiting* and *there would be hell to pay* etc., things that slipped easily off the tongue but which really meant I did not care about these people. I was a schoolgirl by profession, not by choice. I conducted schoolgirl-hood with the diplomacy that I now apply at work.

M and F were expecting me – our family was small and solitary and absences were noted. M and F were both orphans. Orphanhood only seemed appropriate for children or animated animals but that is how F described our family – two orphans and their babies. F because he'd abandoned his religious parents in America and M because her parents were actually dead.

Andrew walked with me to the bus stop. We lived in the same direction.

What if these are the best days of our lives? I asked. One of the teachers had said they were.

Mr. Greene just has a shitty life.

True, he was probably a sad sack at sixteen too. I hated it when adults reminded us that they'd been young. They were predicting our doom.

Andrew laughed. *Don't worry Kit, you'll be extraordinary. You'll fly to Mars and they'll put you in The Museum.*

He was joking. By The Museum he meant the two rooms of town memorabilia that stood next to the now-shuttered tourist information centre. It was where I was about to start working part-time that summer. I'd be doing weekends until school ended, because the tourists were already sun-chasing their way to the sea. Once we finished for the holidays, I'd be there half the week.

The rest of the way home, he described the kraken comic he planned to draw using only blue and yellow ink. I liked listening to Andrew talk. When he told me his plans, I could see them clearly. That was one of the reasons I'd chosen him. Our minds were already so close together that when he talked I could plunge into his ideas. My only doubt was that everyone already thought we were doing it, which made me feel as if the whole year was observing the twists and motions of my body.

We reached my door first and I asked if he wanted to stay for dinner. M liked Andrew because he was polite. F liked Andrew because his love of monsters meant that he listened carefully when F spoke about how baby angels aren't cherubs but putti. Sweet little Italian inventions. And that the cherubim of the Book each have four heads, four wings, ox hooves, human hands and could run thunderbolt-fast. Andrew would nod and draw little sketches and hold them up to F for his approval. The night might have gone better if Andrew had come to dinner and made F smile. But he didn't. He had promised to eat with his own mother.

They say our unconscious minds are always reacting to micro-expressions – the flicker-fast motions that the conscious mind doesn't register but which reveal people's true selves. Our bodies are therefore always having entirely secret conversations with one another. This presents a problem when trying to remember M and F back then. I am tempted to draw what was micro, macro. To paint something far bigger than could be seen on the surface. Because if you'd asked me at the time, I would have told you that everything was fine. Well, not exactly fine, but manageable.

M had cooked a chicken and was carving it on the kitchen countertop, her face level to the bird. Leo stood by her side, chanting, *Wings, wings, wings, wings!* He'd be too embarrassed to do this if one of his mates was over. Nine was too old for dance and clatter in public. Sometimes he seemed unbearably young, shadowing M, and other times he seemed entirely independent of all of us, off in his own secret world of friends and video games.

F put a hand on the top of Leo's head which stopped him. *Wait,* F said, *You have to ask what other people want.* His fingers splayed over Leo's curls, stilling his bounce.

Kit? F asked.

Something in me wanted the slim bones of the wings. Wanted to suck the sweet fat from the joint. I looked at Leo, at the slick of his bottom lip. I considered that he, the miracle child, had somehow got the best of M and F. He had the gold ring around his irises from F and M's delicate jaw. I thought of how I'd had my own room before he was born. F looked at me and he was smiling in a way that said he would support my claim to the wings.

Breast is fine, I said.

Are you on a diet? M asked. *You don't like breast.*

I didn't, it was too bland. And yet, for a moment, it appealed. I planned on becoming the sort of person who lived in the capital and survived on black coffee, grilled chicken breast and green beans. And I didn't want to scrap over a bird. I wanted dinner to be easy, simple. I wanted F to be pleased and for Leo's small fists to unclench.

I really don't care. I filled everyone's glasses because I was thirsty and because it was the sort of house where you were never allowed to just pour your own water.

M inserted the knife into the bend of a leg. Steam sighed out from under the skin. She put it on a plate. *You'll like this better.*

I'll have a wing, F said.

M paused. The knife rested on the chicken's back.

A wing? she asked.

Yes.

Are you sure?

Yes.

Leo sighed.

F looked at M, irritation and something else marking his face, and said, *Leo, you have to share. Now, why don't you put out the cutlery?*

Leo obeyed with a steady *thunk thunk.*

M settled a wing on Leo's plate and a wing on F's. She cut herself a breast. Then for each of us peas, mushrooms in mirin and soy, and brown rice from the rice cooker. On each plate, a blue swallow flew across a china sky. I touched the rim of the plate intended for me. It was warm from the dishwasher.

F went to the fridge to get himself a beer. I moved to take the plates to the table, but M held up her hand to stop me. I watched as M lifted one wing from its plate and tucked it next to its sibling.

For your brother, she spoke quietly, her eyes on F's back. She gestured to the plate of wings. Then she placed a leg where F's wing had once been. I wondered why she bothered lowering her voice. He would notice soon enough.

There is a game that I'd learnt in the playground years before and brought home. The asker says: *If everyone in your family had fallen off the boat and they were all drowning, who would you save?* It could be that in your version it was fire and not water. At the time, Leo had answered honestly, M. I didn't begrudge him that. M said her children. I knew she meant Leo. F refused to answer. I had hoped he'd choose me although I thought he'd pick M – perhaps he had been too hurt that she didn't choose him to say so. Whenever I imagined that boat, I saw our kitchen table upturned – M and Leo on one side and me and F on the other, waiting for the wave to come. I always sat next to F.

I am getting ahead of myself. For the moment, it was me and the split limbs of a chicken, watching as Leo fastened his lips over the narrowest edge of the wing before F had even opened his beer.

I didn't – Leo said when F's eyes found him. The corners of my brother's mouth were stained by dark soy.

He's growing, M said.

F opened the knife drawer too fast and it juddered on its track. *You can't . . . Out in the world, not everything is going to be for him. He's got to learn that.* The bottle opener smiled brightly up from F's tight hand.

Don't, M said.

19

F didn't reply but he jerked the bottle opener so hard the cap span to the floor and rolled under the table, its silver teeth pointing up.

Leo ate fast, gnawing the wings to grey sticks. He even ate the peas and the slime of mushrooms without complaint. F sliced his meat with fork and knife rather than lifting bones to his mouth. I looked down at my own plate. The blue china swallow soared towards the bone of the dead bird.

I have since wondered if things might have been different if I had gone to the park that evening and filled my mouth with the sweetness of cider. Or if I had been the one to ask for a wing. Or if I had taken Andrew to the beach, pressed him against the sand, pushed my face into his and been the sort of teenager that you are supposed to be. Or if none of this had anything to do with what happened next.

The First Night

I'm scared that this next bit will make you dismiss me as an attention-seeker or deranged. You may wonder why you let me into your house, never mind into the warm pocket of your bed. Because of this, I will try to tell it as simply and with as little embellishment as I can. I want you to understand that I was the sort of girl you might have met at your own school. I'm under no illusions of specialness.

After dinner, Leo and I went to our room. Leo got into his bed, under the dinosaur poster. Their bodies with delicately hatched scales had hung in the same place for years. I'd known them so long, I could point to the stegosaurus and apatosaurus through the shadows. Soon, Leo's faint snores rippled across the room.

I sat in bed texting one of the girls on the swim team, gathering up accounts of new dates and new heartbreaks. She was the sort of person whose greatest joy was the pouring out of other people's lives. I didn't like her, but I enjoyed the taste of other people's secrets.

M came to check on us. She was an early-to-bed, early-to-rise person and she was already wearing her pyjamas – rain-grey leggings and a loose tank top that made it look as if she was about to go for a run. She smoothed back the curls from Leo's forehead and kissed him there. Three times, for luck.

She came to my bed and I flipped my phone face down because I didn't like her eyes on the details of my life. She always managed to make them feel small. She looked at me like a patient, like someone in need of counselling.

How was school? she asked in a voice lowered so as not to wake Leo, although nothing woke Leo. He had more than once fallen asleep on a beach towel in the midday sun, with tourists shouting around us.

Fine. Told you at dinner.

Just because exams are over doesn't mean you shouldn't pay attention. This is a good time to talk to your teachers about how to prepare for next year. It felt like she told me these things to simply say them. We had never had that easy repartee that mothers and daughters are supposed to enjoy.

I can deal with next year next year.

You should take advantage of this time, so you don't feel rushed when school starts. You could ask your English teacher what books they'll be assigning you.

English is a pretty useless subject. It's just stories. I didn't mean this. I was taking English further because I liked it. I'd received the highest coursework grade in the year. But there was something about her that always made me want to disagree.

That's not true. It's communication. Communication was a counsellor word. It was one M mentioned a lot. To derail her, I asked her about the small bruise on her elbow. *Caught it getting off the bus,* she said. *This is why you need to use your backpack. Handbags are so uneven, they mess up your spine.*

22

You don't need to make everything into a lesson, I said.

She got up to go to the door. Standing there, she looked over her shoulder and said, *Be polite to Charlie tomorrow if you see him.*

She had a way of reminding me to do the most basic things. What was the point of commanded politeness? Charlie Stenson was the reason we'd moved to the town. He was M's friend from university. She'd once tried to explain the friendship to me like this: *There are two kinds of friends. There are the friends who you always pay back for snacks, for favours, for compliments. Then there are the friends where you both have so much debt that neither of you can account for it.* He'd been the one to see this small house go up for sale, or so the story went. He called M and F and persuaded them to move here from the flat we'd been squashed into since I was barely old enough to remember. He owned the boutique hotel and restaurant that was our town's only claim to any fame. He was also the greatest donor to the museum. He was an unreasonably tall man, as if he had grown in order to look down on the rest of us.

She left through the wedged-open door. Sometimes, I longed for privacy but how that would have been possible in our two-bedroom house, even with the doors locked, I don't know.

I slept.

I woke up on the floor. Nothing new. My head was a little sore. My hip ached where it had hit the boards. Again, I could see Leo in his own bed. And again, I headed downstairs. All I wanted to do was reset my brain so I could return to sleep, go from darkness to light into darkness – such a simple desire.

As I went down the stairs, the sound of M and F talking in bursts preceded my understanding of them. I took a step into the kitchen before stopping.

My father's chair lay on its back, like a woman who'd tilted over in a faint. M had her arms crossed over her body and her mouth pulled into a tight line. F bent over the chair. His hands moved tenderly across it.

M said, *You could've woken them.*

F replied, *I could glue this back together. Or perhaps I could just slot it in.* I saw that one of the spindles had come loose where it met the seat.

I'm serious, Gabriel. You've got to . . . you can't . . . She touched her hand to her forehead. She wasn't looking at me and I backed away into the shadows of the hall.

I'm sorry. I was clumsy.

It's not clumsy . . . She stood as straight as ever and I wondered why she didn't bend down beside him. I tried to understand what he'd done. Knocked the chair? That could have been what had woken me. Things in our house got broken a lot. When F was full of a feeling, he found it hard to keep track of his waving arms. I could see the way he would have stepped back too fast and the chair would have tipped.

F's body curved like a shamed dog and his voice shifted low and angry. *I'm not the babysitter. I get to make decisions about our son.*

I'm going to bed.

You can't always choose Leo. There are other people in this family too. We're supposed to be a team.

M swept past me up the hall. She didn't look at me. I hated her then. Sharp and hard. F was trying to fix the

24

chair. He looked so small and careful. He righted it. I approached. Then he lifted a book from the pile on the windowsill. Books in our house escaped their shelves to windowsills, under beds, the side of stairs.

This was an old favourite – a battered copy of Dante's *Paradiso*. F used to say that it was Dante's unappreciated B-side. Everyone always focused on the *Inferno*, on the death and the demons, the torture, the suicides turning into trees . . . But wasn't it easier to imagine pain than joy? Wasn't the greater challenge to conjure the holy using only mortal words? He opened it to one of Gustave Doré's illustrations – all clouds and wings. The one in which angels swarm bee-like around God. He sat there quietly. Not turning, just looking. His hair falling over his face. At the bottom of the image, two silhouettes stand looking into the brightness of God: one is Dante and the other his guide, Beatrice. F looked at them looking at God. I didn't want to interrupt whatever he was thinking. He didn't move for a long while. He ran a finger over Dante's outline and then Beatrice's.

F? I spoke quietly.

He didn't look over. F, when upset, was better left alone. So I waited longer. He poured himself a single finger of whisky. He sat down on his chair, slowly, carefully, but it held him. He lifted the page. I stepped closer, one hand on the table, waiting for him to look up at me, to shake his head, to say, *Your mother . . .*

He turned the page. He took a sip from his glass.

F? This time it was louder. Sometimes when he went to the cool dark place behind his eyes, I could snap him out of it. Nothing. Perhaps he was disappointed about Sun Songs.

I'm sorry, I'll sing if you want me to. I had never been good at saying *no* to my parents. I was still mastering that teenage skill of defiance for its own sake. I didn't want to sing, but I would if it would make F happy.

He lifted his glass to drink but then, seemingly struck by something in the etching, stopped halfway. His face looked soft, peaceful, a little sad. Still, it was as if he didn't even see me. Andrew's mother, who was an administrator at the local hospital, had taught us the symptoms of a heart attack and a stroke. She'd also shown us how to give mouth-to-mouth and pump a chest, pushing down with all our weight. Afterwards, she'd taken me aside and told me to pee on anyone who tried to rape me, that it might not help but it was worth a shot. Andrew's mum believed in preparing for emergencies. But she had never described these symptoms.

EFFFFFF! It was hard to shout a consonant. The sound jammed in my throat.

No response.

I have rewritten the next paragraph five or six or maybe ten times. Each time I have tried to describe the sweat of fear, it has sounded hysterical, over the top. So let me say that I stood in that kitchen and didn't understand what was wrong. That I waved my hand under his eyes and he did not react. That I followed him upstairs. M was curled on her side. I hesitated, waiting for her to get up and to tell me what was happening. She didn't move. I walked to her and touched her shoulder. She stared at the wall, her eyes not meeting mine. Meanwhile F had stripped down to his boxers. His belly was pale in the half-light. And even then, he ignored me. He moved carefully, lifting the edge of the duvet slowly and slid underneath. I shouted both their names, M and F and their real names, as if I was an acquaintance screaming across a train station. *Reiko, Gabriel, M, F, Reiko, Gabriel.*

Imagine your own parents, the faces you know so well, not responding to you. Think of all the explanations you might come up with, the little shames you would dig up, the ridiculous fears. Now cycle through them for an hour or two, while you look at those faces and they say not one word. Remembering those hours staring down at their bed, the pain and dryness in my throat rises back up.

Eventually, because I couldn't do it anymore, I walked back to my own room. I did not shout Leo's name. I let his huffing body rest. His stuffed lion had fallen to the floor and lay staring up at me. It was then that I saw that my sheets were shaped in the familiar lump of a person. A body.

I didn't scream. I was screamed out.

It occurred to me that this might be a prank by Leo. Though he wasn't really a prankster, too involved in his own dream worlds, but it was possible. Then the body shifted.

My duvet which by daylight had a pattern of stretching cats – M's choice not mine – was a shadow mass. I fumbled for the light but nothing turned on. I stepped closer. At the top of the pillow was a spread of long dark hair. It was a face I knew. It was a face that, to my shame, I had spent a lot of time examining. I would have known it in deeper gloom than this. I had seen it warped by puddles and reflected through foundation-powdered mirrors in the school bathrooms.

The sleeper had my small mole under the lower lash line. M called it a beauty spot. I once read an article that said symmetry was the most beautiful quality in a face. And another article that said beautiful people were more successful. I disliked this mark which might throw my life off kilter. Otherwise, it was just my face. Except now it wasn't.

I pushed my fingers against the sleeper's cheeks. They were soft, but did not give way to my touch. I prodded the sleeper's sternum through the duvet. The sleeper's chest sighed up and down. I shoved it. My hands bounced off. I crawled onto the bed, on top of this imposter. I didn't have a plan, only the exhaustion of having had my eyes open too long and having shouted without being heard. I beat her. I kneed her. I jumped on her with all the power that I devoted to swimming laps at school, slamming against her body the way I pushed off from the tiled side of the pool when executing a turn. The sleeper didn't move, didn't shift, didn't do anything. It was as if I could feel her but she could not feel me. Eventually jumping stopped making sense, the way if you say garage twenty times over it stops sounding like a word at all.

At some point, I stopped fighting the sleeper and pinched a wad of my own forearm the way they do in cartoons. It hurt, but not much. The action felt fake, like I was doing it for a camera, performing the motions that a sane person does when something is not quite real. But I knew the difference between real and unreal. Dreams did not feel like this. My dreams had a simpler horror. The floor would have opened up into a thousand teeth, or the walls would have bubbled with crocodile eggs or I would have failed every exam I took. And if it was a dream, it wouldn't have been so very, very long.

Desperation slid to a slower, quieter panic. This was the panic of the inevitable. It was a panic I would feel many years later after a friend stopped answering my calls. It was the panic I had seen when Leo thought he'd lost his lion and cried for three nights straight before the creature was returned by Lost Property. It was the panic I saw in your eyes when we found out your mother was sick and we rode the bus to the end of the line because you weren't ready to get off. These things do not carry equal weight. But in the dark red moment of panic, the big and the small blend together. Nothing made sense. I lay next to the body with my arms around her shoulders and cried like a hot-faced baby.

At 6.30 a.m., I woke up in my own bed. There was no other body there. None of the night vanished or receded as a dream would.

A Special Star

Years later, a friend of mine apprenticed to study astrology. It's a thing you can actually study, get a certificate in. I didn't tell her what happened all those years ago, but I was still looking for an explanation for why things went as they did, why my mind had not behaved as it should. And I thought that as an astrologer she might be a bit more tapped into the strange. So I asked her to draw my charts.

She told me that I would face many obstacles, though who doesn't? She also gave me macadamia nuts to eat and good strong coffee. So I'm not complaining. She asked me the hour of my birth and I said I didn't know. She asked me the day of my conception and I said I didn't know that either. All I knew was that it happened on a road trip.

M's mother had been born in Kyushu, the southern tip of Japan, and had married a teacher from England who carried her back to his country. Whether my grandmother felt like a souvenir, or an adventurer, I'll never know. My grandparents died one after the other from problems with hearts and brains. M was their only child. After they passed, she took a road trip across America, where she picked up F. At some point on this trip, I took root.

M told me that she'd seen fireworks the night they'd conceived me. That she'd chosen Katherine for my birth certificate, not after the Saint but after the Catherine Wheels – those spinning fireworks that people send up into the sky, as if trying to outdo the stars. It had seemed a bright blessing. I was too young and too embarrassed to ask whether she'd seen them from a muddy field, the lint-seated back of a car or through an open window.

My chart remained inaccurate. The future opaque and the past obstinate. I can't blame the stars for what happened.

The Museum

Excited for your first day at the museum? M asked. She edged her spatula under a piece of eggy bread, flipping it. The buttery-yolky surface gleamed. We called this dish eggy bread, not French toast, because Leo liked things to be called what they were and the bread came from Sainsbury's not France. M was not normally a breakfast-maker. Neither of my parents were. Leo and I did for ourselves from cereal and leftovers. F, if forced to wake early, was slow and silent, glaring at the sunlight as if willing it back to darkness.

I sat in F's chair, trying not to make an exhibition of the choice. I leant into the chair and felt it give slightly but perhaps it always had. I slipped a hand behind my back and ran my fingers over each spindle, feeling for a wobble. The middle one seemed loose in its joint. I bit into my toast. The bread was sweet and good but the little chunks of cooked egg white made me think of eyeballs. My own eyeballs hurt. *Paradiso* lay on the table, the spine wrinkled. Leo clacked his Hot Wheels racer up across the book.

Earth to Kit? M said.

I grabbed the strawberry jam from Leo and dolloped some onto the eyeball-bread. *What?*

Don't be a teenager. M slid her spatula under her own piece of eggy bread to flip it.

I'm just being alive. You're the one who cares that I'm being a teenager. I kept thinking of her sleeping face, deaf to me. Now, it was flushed from working above the hob. A strand of hair stuck to her cheek. I knew she had woken up earlier to do this, for my special first day at work. Her apron was wrapped around her own work clothes. I repented and added, *Sorry. Thanks for breakfast*, M.

Remember to be nice to Charlie. Again. Maybe the museum and its dusty exhibits could have survived off the school carol concert fundraiser and the donation pot that sat on the counter at the corner shop next to the jar for the RSPCA. But with Charlie's backing, I guess they didn't have to.

Doesn't he have a hotel to run? I asked.

We'd all been taken to the museum by teachers who were too bored or too tired to come up with a class plan in those last days before summer. Whelk and lobster pots were examined for longer than seemed possible. We'd stared at the fading photographs of the single famous actor our town had produced. His beaked nose and caddish smile appeared quaint. It was easier to place him in our narrow streets than under the white lights of Hollywood.

Entry was £2.50 for adults and £1 for children. There were pamphlets by the front desk with local walks, local attractions, local restaurants – local again and again, as if the greatest virtue anyone or anything around here had was proximity.

When I first moved to the town, Mrs Hale ran the museum, sitting at the desk doing the crossword over the top of her half-moon glasses and wearing her uniform of thin cardigans. But lately her health had been troubling her and the running of the museum had been taken over by a graduate student from London. Well, she was from Singapore but people appeared more offended that she came by way of London.

Leo, that's enough jam.

Urgh. He sounded so adult. I touched him on the top of his head. His hair was sticky and unwashed. I did the trick with his nose and my thumb. *Stole your nose,* I said. But Leo rolled his eyes, already too old to be amused by me.

Ten minutes later, I put on my jacket with the workmen's pockets that meant I didn't need a bag.

The museum was a fifteen-minute walk away. I moved more slowly than usual, off-kilter. My brain felt overexposed. But my legs and arms moved me easily down the cliff path. The tiredness was only located in the hub of my brain. My feet and hands had been relaxing without me and I looked down at them, betrayed.

The graduate student was there to meet me. She showed me around the museum, which was strange because I'd known it longer than she had. She showed me a laminated ticket from the old bus line that used to run along the coast. I thought of the rumour at school that Mrs Hale's grandson used to bring girls here and they'd blow him on their knees in front of the retired oyster boat engine. As we walked, I imagined the way the carpet would have rasped against their skin.

The graduate student's name was Cassandra Chao. I felt sorry for her, spat out by London to this place by the sea. She was dressed as if people cared what she wore. Her skirt fell to her ankles in complicated pleats. Her nails were painted with small silver moons. She had a nose ring, which M would have said made her look like a cow, but she was more like a lamb. Not the ones you see in paintings, but the ones in the fields around our town who were always escaping through the fences and running into the road or butting their small heads into trees, rocks and the sides of their friends. She spoke sometimes all in a rush and then was oddly silent. She reminded me of Leo when he was playing one of his games of pretend – imitating a fireman or spaceman or policeman. Every now and then she'd pause to look at me to see if I was keeping up. She said *um,* and *does that make sense?* as she explained the working of the till and where the mop was kept. Children had been known to vomit slurries of ice cream onto the floor. I nodded along, all the while thinking of my own body in my own bed and the stiff feel of the cheeks under my fingers.

Cassandra explained that she wanted to update the laminated cards that sat in a box by the desk. She wanted to make proper signs. She had ideas. And while she had those ideas it was my job to dust and take tickets and, if necessary, show people the exhibits. For an un-newsworthy place, we still got a regular helping of Londoners in the summer and after they'd wet their feet and eaten oysters by the beach, many would wander in. They'd laugh at the cheapness of the tickets as if we were mounting some sort of comedy routine. Really, they were the joke – they'd paid to stand in a room of Mrs Hale's old stuff.

Cassandra lodged me at the front desk and went into the backroom to, as she put it, *play with fonts.* Visitors came in – couples who whispered in corners and posed next to the dried puffer fish and families wielding pushchairs that brushed against the framed town maps, wheels clinking against display stands. I searched on my phone when there were no guests in the museum. Some things the internet told me about:

Mind Body Separation: Led to Mind Body Dualism. Philosophers and scientists. Smug articles about the moods determined by your stomach bacteria. Not at all what I was looking for.

Dream travelling: Spiritual awakenings, white wolves, soul transformation. Very different from wandering around your house shouting at your parents.

Spirit walking: Similar. Shamans and vision quests.

Astral projection: Heads with glowing brains. Esoteric books for sale with bright 70s covers, all purple and star spattered. Not the sort of thing I'd be caught dead buying.

Out of Body Experience: Already better. The name frank and clear. *Experience* reminded me of Work Experience or Life Experience.

And so I lingered there on *Out of Body*. I read about people stepping out of their flesh as easily as removing a letter from an envelope. I read about a silver cord that connected your spirit body to your physical body. As I read, I touched the back of my head and felt only hair.

And then I didn't want to think about it anymore. After all, what was one strange night?

I texted Andrew to meet me after work. I thought about when we'd have sex. I imagined us in this room, my own back up against the curve of the boat's engine, my palms pressing against the cool metal and looking down on his

36

dark hair. It was easier for me to conjure up how it would look to have him kneeling before me than how it would feel. I worked on the image for a while.

The imaginary Andrew was so clear that when flesh Andrew walked in, I was startled. An ink stain bloomed on his bottom lip. He stood close to me, leaning on top of the counter.

How's work? he asked.

How's the kraken?

He pulled out a sketchbook full of paper that had rippled from his efforts. He'd written in huge capitals that took up almost the entire front page – *Giant Squid vs The Normans.* And the next few pages were squid arms and little men in fish-scaled helmets who looked like they'd wandered off the Bayeux Tapestry.

They're preparatory sketches. His voice carried hesitance layered with excitement. *It came to me last night – What if William the Conqueror's boat had been squidified?*

That's insane. I held the book carefully so as not to smudge it.

Why? They both came from the sea. Everything would be different.

I didn't like it when our history teacher said that if this or that had happened we'd all be speaking German or not using Latin or whatever. We'd still be speaking, wouldn't we? Would it really matter in what language? But the lines of the cartoon were good and sharp. I liked them. I again thought about his long body under the shirt and the way he moved his hands while he talked as if he was always drawing in the air.

Have you ever sleepwalked? I asked him.

No. But my uncle used to sleep run.

Run?

Apparently. He'd sprint down the road in his bare feet. But when they woke him up, he could never tell them what he was running from.

Flying

After dinner that night, Leo crawled into bed next to me, his feet two cold nuggets. He was always getting into my bed, shoving me over so that the sharp ridge of the mattress pressed into my thigh.

Stop it.

Whatcha watching?

Because it was easier, I took my headphones out and I let him rest his head against me. His hair caught the last of the sun coming in from the window gables. I thought about how the girls at school saved up all month to get highlights put in. He didn't know how lucky he was.

Together we listened to a woman in a smart red dress, with sharp black heels and a PhD, tell us about how she studied out-of-body experiences. She believed they indicated some capacity of the spirit-body not yet accounted for by science. She thought science would recognise them eventually. She called them OBEs, as if giving them an acronym would make them official.

Leo picked at a brown-red scab on his elbow. My brother was always stumbling through the world.

Not in my bed.

What?

No scabs in my bed. It's disgusting.

You're disgusting.

Shh . . . I'm trying to listen.

The woman moved around the stage as she spoke, her palms upturned, her posture welcoming in a studied way. She told her audience that she had become a scientist in order to research an event that happened in her girlhood. She'd flown out of her body and all the way to São Paulo where her uncle lived. She saw him in a bed with a silver colostomy bag and small tubes sticking out of his nose. No one had told her or her mother that her uncle was sick but somehow her spirit-soul had searched him out.

I thought again of my father's hands playing against the frets of the back of the chair.

Where would you fly? Leo asked.

I don't know. What about you?

Tokyo. Or the moon.

The moon? That's pretty far.

It'd be cool though.

Yeah.

He moved closer to me on the bed, leant against me and asked, *It's not real though is it? It's not true.*

On the crown of his head was a small white patch from which the hair grew out in a whorl. I imagined that was where the silver cord would sprout from his body. I touched the spot and he squirmed. I could remember when he was a baby and the plates of his head had barely joined.

I don't know, I said. *I don't know.*

Leo asked, *Would you rather fly or be super smart?*

M came in to tell Leo to brush his teeth and asked what we were watching. I told her a friend had sent me this video and showed her the woman talking. M shook her head and said that sometimes people, especially children,

40

sense something wrong but don't have the logical apparatus to process it. So instead, they dream and see imaginary things and believe they have powers for good or for evil. I played M the bit where the scientist explained that she could not have known, had no way of knowing. And M said that perhaps she had sensed something was wrong in her family and so had had this dream. If she'd dreamt of her aunt and not her uncle it would have been unremarkable. But she happened to be right. It was a bit sad that this dream had shaped the woman's whole life. I pointed out that we'd learnt in school that they thought Louis Pasteur was crazy but now we didn't get smallpox and our milk had his name on it. M told Leo to go do his teeth, now. And Leo said he didn't want to but she shooed him away anyway.

She asked if I understood her job? I shrugged. *Some people's memories are like a swarm of butterflies,* she said, *people who have something bad happen to them, they desperately need to make a story of it, so they keep counting these butterflies again and again and again. They say to themselves, this happened and then this, and then this. But the butterflies keep moving. And they can't keep track. They get so focused on that, that they can't live their present day lives.* She explained that she gave people a story to tell themselves about the butterflies. The story allowed her clients to stop counting. But if people didn't have a therapist they might tell a dangerous story, one that wouldn't help them address the root of the pain. If M had known this woman she might have asked if it made her sad to be so far away from her aunt and uncle and if that was why she dreamt of flying to them. Or why this woman,

41

once-girl, felt that she had to check on the adults in her life.

I told M that she didn't need *to be such a therapist about everything,* which in retrospect was a thing F used to say. I'd never had a therapist and couldn't really have told you what one was like at work. Mostly I meant, don't be so M about it. M sighed and moved my glass of water further from the edge of the bedside table. *You'll spill.*

Later as I lay in the dark, I kept asking myself, *Am I asleep yet?* I touched my knees and my shoulders, checking again and again that it was just me in the bed.

2

I showed you a video of that woman once. It seemed like a way in. A safe place to start. If you didn't laugh at her, then I had a chance. I hoped you might be receptive. That morning you'd been defending people who talk about the weather. *It's not stupid or small,* you said, *the weather affects everyone. Talking to someone about the weather is what you do when you're grasping for something you can both share. It's an act of generosity, you're giving them a question you know they can answer.* And I loved your rage at that invisible and cruel mass of people who forbade weather talk. I was thinking about your kindness when I suggested that we watch the video.

I nodded along as she encouraged the audience to accept without *presumptions* or *preconceived ideas.* The way she said *possibilities* and *possibility* again and again made me ache. I was also worried that you'd ask why I had shown you such a thing. I wasn't ready yet to tell you the whole story.

Then I realised that you'd fallen asleep in my lap. I watched her alone, anchored by your sprawl.

Summer Sea

You've never lived by the sea. In the summer, the sea is a swathe of green-blue that people name fabric colours and jewels after. Summer is when most people spend time by the sea. It's the background they put behind their memories of kicked down sandcastles and sticky sun cream. Easy enough. But I lived by the sea and knew it in winter. I knew it when the sea spray spat into vicious rain. When the waves pulled little dogs under, when the water was not blue but beige because it was churning through the seabed. On wind-wild days, I've edged close to the water as each wave destroyed the last and known that if one caught me, the sea would fling me onto the pebbles until my bones cracked. The scary part is that the summer and winter seas are the same waters.

I would receive my share of wind and waves. But briefly, I thought that this sleep watching and walking might be a gift. Might be a holiday. Might be something fun.

I didn't catch myself tumbling into sleep. I only understood what happened when I woke on the floor again, pressed my hands against the floorboards to lift myself, looked up and saw my body in the bed. It was curled on its side, hands making loose fists. The back of its hair was tangled and matted. I looked at it and found that I didn't want to scream or cry. I knew that I would reattach and

46

find my way back into my bones. It is surprising how quickly the impossible becomes the unavoidable. But I was growing then and so used to change.

I went to the bathroom and looked at myself in the mirror and saw only the tiled wall and the towel hanging on its peg. I looked down and there were my feet sticking out from the flannel pyjamas that M had bought on sale.

I tried jumping, imagining myself floating up, up, up like Peter Pan off to some lost island. It didn't work – perhaps because I was already far too old to believe in fairies. No moon for me. But here I was beyond my body.

I thought of the boys who put a small camera in the vents of the girls' changing rooms. I thought of how it had watched our bodies, mine too, the slabs of flesh, the utilitarian underwear. I thought of how the teachers had found that camera, confiscated it and watched the footage too. How else could they have sentenced the guilty boys? Andrew was not one of those boys who move in a pack. I don't think he saw the video. But maybe he did. I had not seen it. No one showed it to the girls. We only knew that the boys had been punished. After we found out, I often looked at that vent and tried to reconstruct what it had seen. I wondered about the resolution, the angle, what my face looked like as I changed from schoolgirl to swimmer.

How would it have felt to film the boys? If I had seen the line of Andrew's body exposed? I had known his body for five years. The first time I remember registering him, we shared a glue stick. The bones of his face had been hidden under child chub. There was a craze that year for sucking our brushes in art and turning our tongues yellow, blue and redder reds. The whole year's mouths a toxic rainbow.

Even now his mouth was often pigmented by paintbrushes absentmindedly chewed.

It would be easy to get to his house. He didn't live far and I'd taken the route many times before. I walked out of the bathroom, down the stairs and into the kitchen, where F was drying the dishes and muttering under his breath the lyrics to 'Bad Moon Rising'. His hands made a steady swirl. Again, he did not see me. I waved. I now had a name for what was happening and it gave me a kind of peace. I climbed out the open kitchen window onto the slate pebbles that hid the drainage ditch. I landed with no sound.

On the empty street, I felt almost normal. There was no one here to fail to see me. The heat of the day had left the pavement. The road was lit by bedroom lamps, the occasional TV showing a football replay, and the faintest stain of summer sun at the horizon. There were no streetlamps in that part of town. Perhaps there were proposals running through the council. But as I stepped out, I wasn't yet interested in notes the council sent out. The decisions of local government were as distant as Mercury's sweep through the night sky – both happened whether or not I was paying attention.

The way was familiar enough that I only needed the simplest shapes to know where to go. His was the house with the bent-backed, wrinkle-trunked apple tree propped up on a post that was itself splitting with age. I touched the dented brass doorknob. It was wet with condensation from the night or the sea.

It had felt simple wanting to see him, wanting to be near him. I had forgotten about getting inside. Only my house with my nocturnal father and my easily scared brother was so porous. The windows at Andrew's were shut. Even the curtains were drawn. On the ground floor, a yellow light flushed the fabric and I wondered if it was Andrew or his mother inside. It is odd the way people face the appealing side of the curtains inside and bare the plain underside to the street. It is a reversal of the usual pattern – best behaviour being reserved for strangers and ugliness indoors.

I stepped into his flower bed, stepping around the plants, and tried to yank up the window. The window frame was painted and peeling like the side of an old boat. It didn't move. Perhaps it was locked. Or perhaps I was not quite real enough. I reached over to a leaf from the apple tree. It was smooth between my fingers. I pulled but it didn't move and my hands slid away from it. The problem was me.

I thought of the professor in the red dress who soared over São Paulo and how all I wanted was to see my friend. I pressed my feet into the ground and jumped. I slapped back down. Nothing in me soared. But the professor had done more than fly, she had entered her uncle's room. She had passed through walls of glass or stucco and been with him. The least I could do was walk on my own two feet to Andrew. I closed my eyes and walked towards the door. I chose the door, not because it was thinner than brick, but because I was already a person of habits. Walking with your eyes closed is strange enough. You try it. Feel how you become aware of your head bobbing on your neck and of the turn of each foot.

I tried to think of air, of lightness, of transparency. I didn't really know if I was imagining myself immaterial or the world. I didn't know if it would help. My throat felt tight.

I walked.

The moment I passed through, I didn't feel anything. I'd simply taken enough steps and there I was next to the drape of his mother's blue raincoat and his trainers, the laces still in knots where he'd slid out of them. The living room door was framed by a necklace of light. Walking through was easier the second time. Andrew was lying on the sofa wormed around a sketchbook. The page was all claws and eyes and horns – more of his monsters.

His laptop rested open on the coffee table. His gaze swung between the book and the show on the computer.

Seeing Andrew was different from seeing M and F – all families spy on each other. This felt new. His mouth was slightly open, his face loose and relaxed. On the shelf next to the TV, his revision books were stacked, the spines fraying, cotton-bud-white where they had split. More inky monsters crawled across the covers.

His school jumper lay in a snakeskin-tangle on the floor. The dark blue was blotched with black at the cuffs. His phone was beside him. I ran my fingers over it. No light came on. No password was requested. For a moment, I thought the battery must be dead. But no, it was that I was only half here.

I perched on the edge of the sofa where I'd already spent so many hours. His hair was coming to the end of its haircut cycle, falling long around his face. Soon it would be short again and his large ears would make themselves known.

Normally, we looked not at each other, but together at something else – teachers, classmates, the movies of Alfred Hitchcock, photos of Americans who'd received guns for Christmas. Comparing visions. It would be strange to stare at him. But now I could look.

The face was not perfect – it was girlish and scarred by chicken pox. His mouth was unusually small. Still, I liked it. The light in his eyes changed shape. I turned to see the screen. Three figures, one tall and two short, were dressed in white suits like the kind beekeepers wear. They walked across burnt-orange sand. The sky behind them had no clouds. He was using earbuds. Without sound, it was impossible to follow the plot. The tall figure was a woman and the two short ones were a girl and a boy. Their lips opened and closed – faces moving through the motions of anger and love. Sometimes they chased butterflies through the sand and the butterflies were the same dark blue as the desert sky. Nets billowed out behind them.

The episode ended. Andrew clicked to another, looking tired. He was not, as far as I knew, an insomniac. I was grateful he was awake. I let myself lean against him. I had done this before although rarely. The family on the show were getting into their white suits again when I heard the front door open. Andrew pulled out the earbuds, as his mother opened the door from the hallway.

You didn't need to stay up.

It's not a big deal.

Ms Murty had taken her shoes off but she was still wearing her smart coat buttoned up tight. I stood to get out of her way as she sat down next to him. They talked about people I'd never heard of at the hospital. About a

51

crisis of some kind. I had not known administrative crises existed until then.

Want me to warm you some milk? she asked.

I'm good. There's leftover Chinese in the fridge if you want it.

What would life be like in a family of two? If F had been my only parent, would I have told him the strange things that were happening to me? But I couldn't tell M. She'd come up with a rational explanation, and nothing felt rational. Or she'd worry. And sometimes I thought that's all I was to M, a worry.

Ms Murty patted her son's shoulder. As if that was the signal, they both went upstairs. The sense of being an uninvited guest filled me.

I didn't follow him up. It seemed like a line I shouldn't cross. But I didn't leave either. Sometimes, once you have decided to do something not right, it is easier to keep doing it than to stop. I stayed on that sofa next to Andrew's closed laptop feeling peaceful and quiet, guarded by his monsters. I thought I could smell the faint residue of boy smell. Deodorant? Puberty? Someone told me once that you can't smell in dreams, but my nose tickled with his scent.

I lay there until I woke up again inside my skin.

Strangers and Their Homes

The next morning my stomach was unsettled as if my body, rather than my mind, had misbehaved. For breakfast I chose milk-less tea and milk-less cornflakes. Mid-cornflaking, Andrew texted me asking if I wanted to bike down to the cove where we all hung out. It was less known to day-trippers and the sand was usually Cornetto-cone-wrapper-free. I didn't reply. In dream or reality, I had behaved like a stalker. Like a peerer under toilet cubicles.

At the museum, we listened to Cassandra's strange playlist while I scrubbed the floor and cabinets until my hands smelt of artificial lemon. That night I remained within the four walls of our house. It was very quiet. M went to bed early. And F only read. Nothing was broken. The next day, I told M I felt ill. She looked like she didn't believe me, but she was already on her way out the door. And anyway, she knew as well as I did that we were all killing time until summer.

F's phone kept ringing but he always hung up on it. I asked him about the calls while he was making lunch. *You can't have good, fast and cheap,* F said. *Well, that asshole can't anyway. This, on the other hand, is a masterpiece.* He slid a thin, gold omelette onto my plate, jewelled with peas.

The laptop gaped open, screen black, the client's code abandoned. F messed with chords. Wrote in his notebook. Listened to a record. Then strummed more chords.

I was too much of a coward to call Andrew and felt too weird to talk to anyone else. I flicked through some library books and when Leo got home, we watched cartoons and ate whatever we could find in the cupboards.

On the fourth night, I sat on the edge of the bed and patted my body's tangled hair. I was tired. I know that sounds strange because I was asleep. But the feeling was not so different to being taunted by insomnia. There was the same ache of a brain that wasn't resting. I flipped between longing to lie down and wanting to do something, anything. I decided to take a walk. I'd heard the phrase *condemned to walk the earth* be said of spirits and found it strange. Weren't we all condemned to do that? But it seemed better than sitting still.

I decided I didn't need doors and slipped right through my bedroom wall into the neighbour's house. They were having sex on the same Ikea bed that my parents had. I was so startled that I forgot to close my eyes. I hadn't seen anyone fuck before. Embarrassing, I know. It would have been easy to access porn. But I hadn't wanted to, not even the kind that got passed around at school for laughs – men and women in Mickey Mouse costumes or fifty-year-olds dressed up as teenagers. I'd seen film stars slip on top of one another as easily as the penguins in nature programmes poured into the cold ocean. But the lighting of the movies was low and the cameras respectful. You never really saw anything.

Seeing these two in full 3D struck me as almost funny.

The duvet had been thrust from the bed to the floor where it lay next to half full teacups. The couple were retired teachers with the sorts of bodies that rarely feature on the silver screen and certainly not naked. The woman lay on her back with her legs in the air like a beetle while the man inserted himself at angle, lying on his side. They seemed to be having a good time.

I found it hard to imagine myself in either position. I tried to think of Andrew in those roles and that was a little easier. I looked away. I didn't want to be the spying creep again. Men had started to watch me as I walked down the street. To slide into my space. To ask me what I was reading when I sat on the bus. There was no way I wanted to be these men.

I turned away from them and then it occurred to me. The joy of it. Sudden and sharp. No one could see me. Of all the superpowers, the one I'd wanted most was to shapeshift, to be a bird or a cat or even a tree. My feet remained my feet but no one could see them or me, no one was laughing or texting or grading or generally doing the watching that the world does to try to catch you being an idiot. I closed my eyes. I imagined the way long brown deer legs would stretch out under me. I felt the soft flip of a tail. What would a deer do? Run. So I ran. I ran through wall after wall. There was a pleasure in the flick of white paint to pink to wallpaper to white, bedroom to study, sleeping baby to snoring couple. No one laughed that I was a girl and not a deer. No one told me I was too old for games. And so I played at being a dog rolling by the fireplace and a rat crawling along kitchen countertops. It felt almost like freedom.

I ran until I found myself in yet another stranger's bathroom. This one was small. There was no cabinet and bottles grew coral-like all around the bathtub and loo. A woman sat on the edge of the tub holding a metal tube of cream. She dabbed this cream across her belly. The skin was creased, mottled and red. There was a boy in my year who had eczema but I didn't know him well. I'd never asked him about the shifting continents of red. The woman applied the cream slowly – squeeze, dab, small circle of the fingers. She did it with such care. It was the motion of a person who believed they deserved gentleness. I could see that. The finger stroked each nub and bump. There were places where the skin was lifting off the body, each flake had the translucence of a ladybird's wing. It felt good to watch her. To look different, to have your flaws show on your skin, these were the worst things that could happen to a girl. This rule was so simple that I'd never heard anyone say it, but I knew it. And yet this woman's face was not ashamed.

I sat down next to her on the edge of the tub. I let my head fall onto her shoulder, there seemed no harm in it. I did not know her, would never see her again, we were strangers. I let myself be rocked by the woman's shoulder and its steady rhythm as she applied the cream. I closed my eyes and for a while, I was just a girl living. Not asleep. Not awake.

A Clean House

A few confused days passed. I couldn't skip every class I had with Andrew. But I made my excuses not to linger as we usually did. In the night, I walked and spied but never on people I knew. I pretended that I was just dreaming.

Again, my spirit swung up from my body, as easy as getting out of bed. The flutter of my parents' voices wafted up the stairs. Children are spies by instinct. You must have done the same – eavesdropping. It's how you get some idea of the future. I didn't hesitate before going downstairs. Both were in the kitchen. M sat at the table, while F was doing the washing up. His pink gloves dipped in and out of the bubbles. M tugged her teabag in circles around the cup. *I don't see why you won't do it.*

I can't. F clattered a fork between its friends.

What he's offering is more than fair. We could do with it.

The sponge squeaked against a mug.

M continued, *It'd be a fun summer project. He's your friend.*

Not my friend, F said, his back to M, *Your friend.*

It wouldn't even be difficult. He just wants an update to guest check-ins. It won't be hard.

F ran the hot tap and the sound of it filled the small room. I leant against the doorframe. It felt almost natural.

I'm busy, F said.

With what? M frowned. I didn't keep track of F's clients but I knew he'd quit a big job that spring due to what he'd called *artistic differences.*

F rinsed a fork clean and held the tines up to the light. *There's this song. I can feel it at the edge of my brain. It's so close but I can't quite . . .*

Maybe you're overthinking it. You've been too much in your head.

F plunged his hand into the water again, pulling out a glass that squeaked as he ran the sponge over its surface. He did not reply. M frowned and added, *We could sign Leo up for that evening drama class if you did it. You know his school has basically no theatre.*

The secondary did but in class productions I was the girl in black moving props. The only time I was heard was when a heavy table slid from my hands to the floor.

Leo is a child. After-school is for daydreaming. Children are supposed to be bored. They're supposed to kick around behind the supermarket parking lot talking a big game about becoming actors. They're not supposed to sit in a dusty room with some failed drama student telling them how to be trees.

I laughed but no one looked up. I thought if I was solid, he would catch my eye to say, *you understand, don't you?*

M plopped the tea bag onto the edge of her plate. Stained water blended with biscuit crumbs.

It's not just the drama classes. What was the last project you actually finished? Go down the pub with Charlie, hear him out.

I need to get the melodic line right. I don't expect you to understand but you could support me.

I do support you, but we're a family and maybe consider . . .

No, F said in the voice he normally reserved for Leo.

M pinched the bridge of her nose. *I don't know why you're being like this about it.*

He turned to her, still wearing the pink marigold gloves. Soap clung to them, the bubbles shimmered.

He reached out in the direction of the biscuit plate. M opened her mouth to say something else, and the hand swerved, landing on her pale grey cardigan. His rubber fingers pressed against her shoulder. Bubbles slid down the rubber and popped on the knit. A watery darkness slipped from his palm into the wool. The gesture was slow. His hand was dripping with dirty liquid. The glove stayed there, his fingers denting the fabric.

M moved as if to twist away or to turn to look at him, but the hand pinned the shoulder to the back of the chair. A bubble popped, making a sound like a kiss.

I said no. F's tone was quiet and careful. His hand didn't move.

Stop it. There was a pleading in her voice that I hadn't heard before. An ache. It was familiar only because I'd heard it in myself and in Leo. *Let go. That fucking hurts, Gabriel.*

I knew my parents bickered. This was something all parents did. M repeated herself too often and F was always

59

forgetting when it was his week to go to the shops. I was used to their squawking. It had not occurred to me that there was more. The wet patch grew darker. The word *Liars* ran around my head, though I couldn't have told you what exactly the lie was.

I've thought about this moment since. Wondered at my slowness – how I stood and could barely see my own thoughts. I don't think I was scared for M then. She was always so in control. Remembering it now, I imagine the crackle of fear she must have felt. But at the time, I was filled with a wet, wordless feeling – the way I imagine the land feels when it is flooded.

He lifted his hand.

M touched the spot where it had been, lifting the fabric and looking down at the damp mark. Her face was stiff. She stood and walked out of the room. F returned to the washing up. There was a care to it. His hands moved in gentle circles over each of the plates.

F began to hum. It was his Sun Song – though something about it had shifted. Some note had been rearranged. There was a pining to it. He collected M's cup and her plate from the table and dipped them into the warm water. He did not rush upstairs to apologise or explain. He braced his hands against the edge of the sink and stood leaning towards the swan neck of the tap. He was motionless long enough that I had time to notice his reflection, a single line on the stainless steel.

The Marigold gloves made a suctioning noise as he pulled them off. He eased them into their spot behind the sink. They lay one on top of the other as though they were praying.

F's guitar was against the wall. He picked it up. The song grew chords. I wondered if this was what it would feel like to be dead? When we die, will we have to look helplessly on? No wonder ghosts in stories are furious. I had a poltergeist-vision of throwing the plates to the floor and watching them smash into a thousand pieces, as if I could tell him to get up and undo whatever it was he had done. I reached for a plate from the rack and my fingers slid off the surface as if they were buttered. Each plate was a different charity shop find. We had a Diamond Jubilee Queen Victoria mug, simply because F liked the way the Queen seemed to be rolling her eyes. I tried again. Again my fingers slid.

This song was soft. Other girls at school had mentioned that I had a cool dad. A girl I now avoided used to tell me she thought he was *fuckable,* emphasising the *f.* It annoyed me because I knew that she meant it. Other fathers were obscured by their middle-agedness whereas he was a boy who had been left out too long in the sun.

I held my arm out straight at the shoulder. I wound it all the way back and then with all the force I had, I swung it towards the dishes. My hand moved fast, in a sweeping blur. It bounced back. I felt nothing. The plates did not fall. The water molecules continued along the route gravity set them. His song lilted on.

Stone Fruit

The next morning, M was emptying out the dead light-
bulb drawer. She collected the bulbs to take to the
recycling centre in town.

Your dad says to come straight home after work. He
wants you to help him at the garden centre. Her voice
was calm as if nothing had happened the night before.
But I was sure that I had not been dreaming. It had
been too detailed, their faces too unerringly their own.
No one had turned into anyone else, no one had got
into a hot air balloon and flown away, no one's hands
had twisted into claws. And yet, I might have preferred
claws.

Why?

One of his schemes.

Our garden was a long strip of green at the back of the
house that ended in the tangle of a hedge. Neither M nor
F were the type to keep aphids off the roses.

Kay.

The museum was fine. Cassandra had me wiping down
the deep diver mannequin, running a moist cloth underneath his plastic eyes and over the folds of his stiff lips. As
I worked, I distracted myself by imagining cleaning under
Andrew's curled black lashes and around the dips at the

edges of his mouth. I dusted the oyster boat engine and thought about the boat game. If we truly were all lost in the storm, M would swim herself to shore.

I heard a yowl from Cassandra's office. She was surrounded by cardboard boxes. The people of our town often gave Mrs Hale their things when they died. Things no child and no jumble sale wanted. Flyers for takeaways that didn't exist anymore, old postcards they'd failed to sell and even children's shoes scuffed at the edges. I suppose people had decided all of it was history. Cassandra leant over an open box.

Rat? I asked.

She laughed and shook her head. I peered over to see a magazine, bleached and wrinkled by the years or sea air. The girl peeking up at the viewer through a fringe of false eyelashes, was displaying an ample rack.

Don't look, you're underage, Cassandra said. She sounded more amused than concerned.

I'm fine.

She flipped the flap shut, using the tip of her boot, making a show of it.

It's about lunch time don't you think? she said.

We ate our lunches together – her a wilted salad and me left-overs heated in the grease-browned staff microwave.

You know what's funny? Cassandra asked.

Mmm?

Housewife porn. It seems kind of sweet now. The most daring thing they could think of was a fully grown woman fucking her plumber. No fisting, no distressed schoolgirls, no barely legal. She had a look on her face as if she knew she was being shocking and wanted to see how I'd take it.

Her eyes were large and bright behind her huge silver-framed glasses.

You're going to add an adult corner to the museum? I'm sure that'll delight Charlie.

She offered me a spoonful of roasted chickpeas and I shook my head. I thought about how I still hadn't replied to Andrew. When I prepared to imitate my normal self in text form, I felt exhausted. My mind was too fuzzed to produce the easy teasing tone that let him know I cared, but not too much.

F was already sitting on the hood of the car when I got home. He was drinking coffee. I knew without looking in the mug. He always found being awake in the day challenging. As if he was a different sort of animal than the rest of us, built to rise as the sun sank.

Garden centre closes in an hour. He put the mug down on the front wall. Leo was already in the back seat playing one of his games, his face a knot of concentration.

When we were on our way, I asked, *So what're we doing?*

Buying your mother a yellow plum tree.

Why?

I was reading an article about the temperatures in England changing. They're growing champagne grapes in Hampshire and Kent, you know that?

I thought about the mug he'd left on the wall. Would ants drink the dregs? Would it keep them awake, if ants slept at all? I asked, *Did you always have problems sleeping?*

He turned the radio on. He liked to have music even if you were talking to him. *Since I was about two years younger than you.*

Anything ever helped?

He overtook another car, slipping fast in and out of the lanes. *No speed cameras until the next junction,* he said and then, *Yes. I suppose. I know you've never been to where I grew up but there were a lot of churches. They each had their own huge parking lots, with signs saying only members of the congregation could park. Worship got you both a place in heaven and a place for your car. And the parking lot for the one we went to was right across the street from where we were living. Right at the back where the lot met the church there was a hump of grass, a patch they'd missed when paving over the whole thing.*

F had a way of storytelling like he was narrating an inner vision. You say I have the same way about me sometimes, so you'll understand that it's alarming when the person behaving this way is driving. All the same, I wanted to know what he would say.

Sometimes I slept out there. On that patch, I mean. And I always slept well.

Because of the church?

I suppose. You know they build them with spires to represent the finger of God pointing up to the sky to tell you that's where He is.

Yeah. It was one of his favourite facts.

I liked seeing how small the spire was against the stars. It reminded me of how small their God was with his opinions on buttoning your top button and sinful music and how much bigger my God was than theirs. How theirs was only up in the sky and watching who they fucked while mine was vibrating in the electrons of sinners and electric guitars and, well, everywhere.

Why did you stop sleeping there?

I moved.

But there are churches here . . .

He didn't answer because we'd arrived. The trees were at the very back next to body-sized bags of gravel and ornamental pots stacked paper-cup style. The saplings looked narrow and uncertain. Their leaves were wider than their trunks.

F told me to look for a yellow plum. I flipped labels, swivelling each to read the backs. Some were smart with images of fully grown trees, giving advice about positioning, but others were a sharpie scrawl. Leo was too short to reach the tags and anyway he was still playing the game on his phone. It was really only for M that he was the miracle child. There were no plums at all. Not purple. Not red. Not yellow.

Aren't any, I said.

Must be.

Why plums? I asked as I read: bird cherry (*Prunus avian*), black cherry (*Prunus serotina*), crab apple (*Malus sylvestris*), and pear (*Pyrus communis*).

For your mum.

Why? Maybe we should ask for help?

Adults have to have some secrets. You go. Leo and I will keep looking.

The woman in her green vest with her official name tag followed me to F and inspected all the labels that we'd already read and told us that *yes, there were no plums,* that *really you wanted to plant a plum in the winter anyway when the plants were sleeping.*

F stood and he looked at her and I looked at him and Leo looked at his game and overhead the gulls were fighting. F didn't say anything. His disappointed silence was heavy next to me.

She started asking about what type of soil we had which I didn't know. I didn't know how you would begin to know that. I still don't. For both her sake and for F's, I didn't want her to notice his silence, so I said that the front of our house faced the coast and the garden looked inland. We weren't shorefront but we were close enough to hear the sea. And the woman made guesses about chalk and lime. I looked over her shoulder. There was no one there my age, so I squeezed F's elbow nudging him to react.

But you don't have any plums? I said again.

We have other lovely fruit trees. She gestured a gloved hand at the display. *We have an apricot, they're a little like yellow plums.*

I guess. I looked at F. *Dad?* I called him Dad in front of other people because I had learnt to mimic a normal family.

He looked at me.

Dad? I repeated.

He seemed to brace himself and then he smiled. F smiled not with just his mouth and his eyes but with his shoulders dropping and his ears lifting – a full body smile. He could make that shift when he wanted you to feel appreciated.

The apricot tree fitted in the back of the car, although the branches jounced against Leo's face.

Why does Kit always get to sit up front? he asked through the thicket of twigs.

Because she's older and she helped.

It's not my fault I'm short.

67

You didn't try. You know, those games are designed to make you feel like you're achieving something or making something but you're only consuming, right?

So? Leo kicked his legs against the back of my chair. The *thunk thunk* dancing up into my spine. And while I didn't know if I agreed with F, I didn't defend Leo. F played the radio and it didn't have any words but we both hummed along. In the back of the car, the branches jigged. I thought about what M had said about how sometimes our brains make up bad stories, untrue stories. I thought about how no one knew if out-of-body experiences were real. I thought about how everything might, after all, be fine. His easy favour washed over me in the car despite Leo complaining and leaves tickling the back of my neck. Even now when I try to summon the feeling of being loved, I always hear F's humming and mine intertwining.

You're my favourite person now. I don't know if I'm yours. I'm afraid you'll say I'm *one of* your favourite people which isn't the same thing. Yet, I hope you enjoy knowing that you're mine.

By the time we got back it was too late to plant the tree, so we hid it behind the bin shed.

Lucid Dreams

Sometimes when I've begun to tell people about those dreamless nights, they tell me about lucid dreaming. They say that if you practise, it is possible to lucid dream. These are dreams you control with your mind. You can summon pet unicorns, build yourself a tree house or fly around a city playing DIY Grand Theft Auto. This was the opposite. I controlled only myself and barely that.

F sang.

M worked. I peered over her shoulder close enough to see the details of her clients. Sad shorthand about teenagers with terrible lives. *Mother. Esteem. Lonely. Boyfriend. Consenting?* I wondered how often she was thinking of these other families while she was with us.

Leo snored.

F strummed.

Once F stood too close to M so that she backed up against the kitchen countertop, the side slicing into her.

Once M took small white tabs of arnica. Boots' own brand label.

Once M sat very still on the edge of her bed with her eyes closed, not moving at all.

M slept.

F slept.

I hadn't been counting the nights but soon it was the end of school. At the final assembly, there were the wrong number of prizes, too few for everyone to receive one but enough that those who didn't felt a little sheepish. Everyone was fiddly, half-bored, half-nervous. I received a ten-pound book token for the best English coursework. We were reminded that, *even in the summer you are representatives of the school*. From the back whooped a sarcastic cheer.

I wandered further. More strangers. Bodies unrecognisable in darkness. Some friends illuminated by their screens. A girl from swimming eating cold baked beans from the tin, the lid curling like a single petal. Her eyes looking off to nowhere as she ate. My maths teacher wanking, his shoulders sloped. I was glad I would not have him again the next year.

There was beauty too. Cats, their eyes green and yellow, ground-borne stars. Sometimes they seemed to see me. Moths that flicked shadow-winged through the night. Frog song bubbled up. Perhaps if I'd stuck to looking in wild places things would have been different.

Merwomen

I sat on a rock, the sea at my back, while Andrew sketched me. From this perch, I could see the way the church spires cut splinters into the sky. I pictured God skimming a hand against each one.

I'd suggested that we meet up. Avoiding him had felt important until it hadn't. Splitting off from myself might be a thing that I and a red-dressed professor had in common. But perhaps it wasn't really happening and I could release the ugly feeling I got when I looked at those pink rubber gloves. Although if that was true, I could no longer trust my mind. I wanted to gather evidence. Collect it. Collate it.

If Andrew had any sense that I'd been hiding, he didn't mention it. He just asked if I would mind posing as a merwoman. And I'd complied. I didn't bother asking if it was for the kraken comic or one of the other magical worlds he set in and around our town. I'd been many people in his drawings – half-spiders, rat-girls, dead bodies, ghosts. Being looked at by Andrew never made me self-conscious. I didn't worry if he'd make me attractive or curvy or lanky because he was always throwing a disguise over me.

I used to relish drawing. Starting a picture felt like gulping down possibility. But after meeting Andrew, drawing felt foolish. My proportions were not as accurate. My hand was more uncertain. He hadn't suggested I stop. But he used to tell me I was a writer. That the drawings I made were really a form of note taking, of observing. *You don't think in terms of the composition, Kit. They're more, um, visual memos,* he'd said when I asked him why my drawings never worked. Maybe he was right after all. This is the longest thing I've ever written. I wonder what he'd think if he knew?

The hairs on my arms rose up from his gaze or from the cold air. We talked as he drew. I'll never have the capacity to sit good-model still. The fidgets creep into my hands too easily.

Look at the sea again will you? Andrew pointed as if I didn't already know where the sea was. I thought back to sitting invisibly beside him in his room. I tried to remember what had been on the screen.

Watching the sea eat itself, I let the words out, *I saw a clip of some show with butterflies in it. And I think two kids and their mum? But I can't remember the name. Do you know the one I mean?*

Mmm, he said. *Maverick scientist? World burnt out by global warming?*

I guess. I only saw a picture. There's a desert?

Yeah. It's about how only the corporate-educational-complex owns the patents for effective sun protection and she's trying to make a new one out of butterflies to save her son's life.

That sounds cool.

I like it. Can you tilt your head up?

The sound of the sea overpowered the scratch of his pencil. Staring out at the horizon, it was impossible to see him or to see what he was doing. The waves gulping each other down made me think of the wet patch on M's shirt. Because I didn't want to think about that anymore and because it was easier to talk without looking at him, I said, *I had a dream about you the other day.*

It is true that people find dreams boring but the exception is dreams that are about them. He kept his pen close to the page, tip moving. I kept talking.

I dreamt that I visited you in the night and you were watching that show. It was actually a bit dull really, you watched it, your mum came home and then you both went to sleep. I felt the heat of the lie rise into my cheeks as I said *dream.*

You dreamt about TV? Weird.

Another girl from our year, Elise, appeared. She was on the swimming team with me. Always the fastest, other than last year when she'd been suspended. It was because she'd stopped eating, the rumour went, not to please boys or fit into clothes but to streamline herself, to turn herself into a water-bound arrow. Her punishment was that they took swimming from her for three months and we lost every tournament. She came back. We assumed she was eating. Her hair was sea-bleached now, and she wore the long green suit of our swimming uniform. More mer-girl than I'd ever be.

She waved to us, hand high in the air, and we waved back. She dropped her towel on a rock and ran into the sea, feet flipping skywards.

Gannet

I saw Cassandra and Charlie through the museum's window. He was behind the ticket desk with her. Their backs were to me. Her laptop was open, presumably to all those fonts. She was sitting down and he was standing over her.

Charlie's finger touched the screen and left behind a smudge.

A friend of M's from uni came to stay once and in a tipsy giggle confessed that she'd always thought M and Charlie would end up together. That M was the only person who Charlie really trusted. It was strange that this tall man would be afraid to trust. But I was too young to understand that everyone's inner lives lie tangled with things they'd rather no one see.

I watched him with Cassandra. His back curved over hers reminded me of the bent backed heron on the Sea Birds of Britain Poster that hung near the museum entrance. I felt almost night-invisible. I made as much noise as I could shoving open the door.

Morning!

Morning Katherine. Charlie fixed me with his salesman eyes. *How're you liking it down in the mines?*

It's alright.

Paying you well? It was a Charlie sort of joke. We both knew that the person who was paying me was essentially him. I'd known that when I applied for the job – known it was wrong to hope I might get it because M used to dance with me while F's band played and Charlie stood holding her drink. She spun me around and around and around. And I would see him smiling over her shoulder.

Great, I said.

Saving up for anything special?

Uni.

Clever girl. Charlie smiled again. *Tell your mum and dad I said hi, alright?*

I told him I would. And I thought of the job that F would or would not do for Charlie. I imagined him standing behind F's back, touching F's computer, which we were never allowed to do. And it was like someone finally turned off a leaky tap in the back of my head and the slow drip, drip, drip of something not being right stopped. I understood why F had been so upset about M wanting him to work with Charlie. Charlie's hands poking and touching F's computer might feel as dirty as dishwater. He hadn't been trying to hurt M – only to convey how he felt.

Charlie left and Cassandra beckoned me to take his place. On screen there was an illustration of a cliff being nibbled from underneath by the sea. Above it the title **COASTAL EROSION!**

Help me pick a font. This one's boring. And this one – it's maybe too cute. She flicked down a menu: sans serifs to serifs to dodgy serial killer writing. *And Charlie likes that one but it's a crime. What do you think? You're young. You're cool.*

I don't know about cool.

You don't like any of them.

They're fine.

I remembered that someone's dog had died falling off the crumbling edge years before. Our class had lit tea lights on the sand. The wind kept blowing the flames out as if the whole beach were its birthday cake. And I remembered wondering how the dog must have felt when ground became not ground.

You okay? Cassandra asked.

Yeah.

You sure?

I nodded. Cassandra span around in her chair. And looked me in the eyes. *I have a little sister.*

Okay?

And this is what I'd say to her if she were making that face. There are people who get eaten by their demons and people who bite back. Be a demon eater. She bared her small white teeth at me. There was something in the way she said demons that I might have believed that she meant real ones. I imagined her spooning up horns and scales with her salad fork. Something unclenched and my laugh came out loud and wild and I only stopped myself when I saw with embarrassment a tiny fleck of saliva flying through the air.

Good. That's better, she said. *Now go figure out why the map display smells of old fish.*

Watering In

The apricot tree languished by the bins for ages. M never spent much time in the garden so I didn't think she'd see it. But eventually F seemed to remember. It was a no-museum day. F fed Leo and me his signature fried-egg sandwiches for lunch. I picked up the last flakes of salt from the plate with the pad of my finger. F said, *I was thinking by the window, where we'll be able to see it. Want to help?*

Leo asked, *Do I haaaave to?*

I'll do it, I interrupted. Others in our year complained about helping their parents, but most of F's chores were fun, learning how to restring a guitar or pressing record and stop on his computer while he was working out lyrics.

F had got the spade out and chosen a spot. He had me read from the phone as he dug.

Dig in one bucketful of well-rotted organic material . . . dig in?

They mean add rotting stuff to the hole. Drag that compost over.

The bag was heavy and I could feel it pulling on my shoulders and elbows, fighting me even over the short distance. When I had almost reached him, he took the bag and tore it open with the fork. Soil tumbled out. He bedded it in, the rusted edge of the spade cutting runes in the earth.

It says here that you're supposed to plant between November and March, in dormant season, I said. It was June.

F leant against his spade. He was breathing heavily. His arms had typing muscles and guitar muscles, long and lean – they weren't spade muscles. He looked at the sapling. The breeze lifted and dropped the leaves. I thought about the tree being awake. I wondered if a tree had ever had an out-of-body experience in winter and flown across grey skies. How far had it travelled? It had a whole season while I had only night. Now that it was awake, could it sense us?

We could keep it behind the bins until November? I said.

Not enough soil, he said. *That woman. It's a cheat, selling trees you can't plant.* He looked so upset that I didn't remind him that she had mentioned a dormant season for plums and weren't we the idiots for not asking about apricots?

It'll probably be fine, I said, not because I knew that it would be fine but because we'd already dug a hole deep enough to bury my head inside.

We kept going. I held the trunk of the tree, my fingers wrapping around it so my index met my thumb and he pulled the plastic pot. The soil that emerged was a perfect mould of the pot clutched by thin white roots.

I consulted the phone. *We have to break up the root ball, but be careful of the taproot,* I said and then, *What's a taproot?*

It's like the carrot. Good. He levered the plant slowly to the ground.

The carrot?

He worked his fingers into the soil. His face had the same peaceful expression it did when he was singing to himself.

The taproot is the first root that leaves the seed, it's the thickest and it goes the deepest. So the carrot is the taproot of the carrot plant. And all the little roots are its side roots.

We're looking for a carrot?

He explained that we weren't, just a root longer and stronger than the rest. I crouched down next to him and hooked my fingers into the white web, pushing out dirt and small pebbles. I loved the warmth and the tick, tick of pebbles hitting the ground. We worked side by side.

Some time passed, the ball became looser, roots frizzing out to the sides. But no taproot.

Loose enough, he said.

I was disappointed not to feel the life of the tree in my hand. Though later someone told me that many nursery-grown fruit trees arrive with broken taproots – in moving away from their birthplace they lose their deepest connection, too.

My phone trembled with messages about nothing much. When I checked them, dirt smudged the glass. We planted the tree, packing the new soil around the roots, until the only thing left was to water it in. I said I'd fill the watering can. Leo was in the kitchen, lining his raisins up on the table in some secret game. I dipped the watering can under the tap. Over the sound of the water, I heard

M's car come up the drive. I had a thought – this might be an apology for the Marigold gloves fight. And I wanted this new green possibility. For my father to be a man who planted my mother trees and for my mother to be a woman who loved them. I was careful not to slosh on the floor.

M's here. I told him. *Maybe she could water it in. It would be a bit like how celebrities cut ribbons at the opening of supermarkets.*

He grinned and I knew he approved. We went inside to greet her. She was taking off her shoes in the hall, but he told her not to.

F took M by the hand and led her out the back door into the garden. Leo and I followed behind. She and the tree were around the same height. He'd pulled her so close that the leaves almost touched her face. They were eye-shaped, green staring in every direction. M examined the tree with her head tilted. In her silence, I noticed how we'd left the plastic pot turned over on its side and the way the grass was dirtied where we'd shaken out the knot of roots.

It's an apricot, F said. *We'd wanted yellow plums, but this is pretty close.*

M smiled with only her lips. *It's lovely.*

It was supposed to be a surprise, I added because I wanted her to say thank you. I wanted her to know how unhappy he'd been when he thought we might fail. How much he wanted this for her. I lifted my hands to show the dirt underneath the nails.

A full fat silence had poured over the garden, covering us all and blocking our throats. F was still holding her hand and while I had been talking, his grip had tightened. He was using the same hand he used to grip the neck of his guitar. It was a strong hand, one that could hold on for hours. Within that grip, M's fingertips were pressed together tight and close and pink like the petals on a rose bud. I could see his wedding ring. Gold and plain. It seemed like the ring would hurt, pressing down on her fingers like that. I imagined the sharp edge of metal against my hand.

I willed her to speak, to say something because then F would let go and laugh or maybe put his arm around Leo so we could all take a group picture with this new green family member. I pinched soil out from under my fingernails and it disappeared into the grass.

M? I said. She wasn't looking at me or at her hand or at the tree but somehow through us all.

Then Leo, who had been using the tip of his toe to dig into the earth said, *Do you like it? Kit didn't know. But I thought you would like it. You like it don't you?*

That's not true. I never said that. You were playing your game the whole time. You didn't even help dig the hole. I hated myself as I spoke, I didn't want to degrade myself by fighting with Leo and anyway, though I hadn't said it, I also hadn't been sure that she would want this skinny little tree.

M jerked free of F and pulled us in toward her. *It's a lovely tree. Thank you all. Maybe we can make apricot jam next summer.*

And then she glanced up and across at F and said, *I'm going to be working Saturdays starting next week.*

What? Leo and F protested at the same time.

I was getting more requests than I could fill, and this way you can all spend more quality time together. Who knows, by next year we might have an orchard.

Leo shook his head from left to right to left and back. *Don't want an orchard.*

M bent down towards him. *Yes, but grown-ups have to be a team. And your father needs more time to spend on his song. So I'm going to work a little bit harder.*

They went inside. F picked up the spade and the fork and threw them into the back of the shed where we kept our bins. They clattered loudly as one hit the other. I picked up the full watering can and turned the earth black.

M

When I split that night, M was standing by me. She skimmed a hand over the cotton of my duvet. She stared at me. My body lay there, lungs inflating and deflating, letting this happen. It felt odd that she could not see me watching her, watching me. The only sound was the wind coming off the sea. I may be imagining it now, but I remember the wind was stronger that summer than in the years before. Her hand moved and it touched where the bedsheet rose under my body's foot. I curled my own foot, as if to pull away. It felt wrong that the body's foot lay perfectly still. She stood like that for a while. Her hair was wet from the shower and lay heavy over her shoulders. Then she turned and walked out.

I followed her and she stopped at the top of the stairs. From below came F's song. Changed again, faster now, less a lament, more frantic. It was strange to me how the same song could shift slightly and become something else entirely. She paused. A step one way and she'd go downstairs and another and she'd go to her bedroom. She thought something, though I don't know what. I just watched it set her muscles in motion as she descended the stairs. She was not the only one who could look. In the kitchen, she asked F if he could run the washing machine before he went to bed.

She used his name, *Gabriel*, the way she used ours when we weren't paying attention.

I'm sorry it wasn't a plum, he said.

It's fine.

He sent a hand twanging over the back of his guitar.

It's lovely, she said. It didn't sound convincing.

I miss dancing, he said.

I tried to remember what M and F looked like dancing. At concerts F was always playing or preparing to play or recovering from playing or standing in the back with the rest of the band judging the other performances.

M nodded, in a way that looked less like agreement and more like acknowledgement. She picked a stray spoon up off the counter and slotted it into the dishwasher. F put down his guitar and stood up.

Dance with me, he said.

There's no music. Her voice was the one she used to tell us not to dawdle, not exactly angry but brisk.

He reached for her hands and she flinched back. But he caught her anyway and pulled her into a waltzish stance. I don't know what era it was supposed to be from. They rocked in the kitchen. Outside, the wind was monologuing. And they were pitching from side to side. Faster and faster. Her face changed shape, from flat, to annoyed, to something else. His hands were not around her hands but at her wrists.

Let go, she said.

Come on, he said, *dance with me*.

No. And she began to move, her body octopusing in the air, twisting in a way that if set to the right soundtrack might have been a dance or a thrash. And F was standing over her and holding on and his feet had stopped moving and he was still holding her. Her face was all fight, it was like Leo when he wouldn't do his homework or eat his broccoli. That's the curse of families, I suppose, the resemblance. Nothing is ever just itself, is it?

And F saying, *Why are you being so dramatic?* But not letting go. There was something wrong about the scene because it was M who looked angry, her cheeks pulled tight under the eyes. While F who was holding her looked hurt.

Let go. M was stage whispering, her mouth full of wind.

And then F was kissing her. I know some people's parents fawn over each other in public. But M and F were not like that. I saw them kiss only on New Years and birthdays. His face pushed close against her. Her arms moved again and this time they ended up caught straight out. They stood as if crucified. Then her arms went completely limp, like fish that had finally been out of the water long enough to die. And the kiss ended. F let go. Her lip was cut to reveal a shining crease of blood. She rubbed it with the back of her hand and it blurred across her chin.

Don't, F said. Though I didn't know what he was telling her she couldn't do.

Shush, she said. *You'll wake Leo.*

I don't know if you can understand this, but all I wanted was to turn my brain off, even for half an hour, even for ten minutes. I turned my back on them and walked upstairs. I curled up on the free sliver of my bed next to my body. I remembered the blog post that talked about the spirit getting in and out of the body as easily as pulling a letter out of an envelope. I touched the body's warm shoulder. I pressed down on her cheek. It did not move but I felt the roundness of it and the bone underneath. I thought about how normally when I touched my own skin it was hard to parse what was my cheek feeling my fingers and what was my fingers feeling my cheek – the two sensations overlapping and indistinguishable. My cheek, the ridge of bone under the softness of skin, was alien. Then lying down next to that body, I tried to forget about bone and skin and its separateness. I closed my eyes and tried to see myself sliding inside my skin until I did, a letter pushed back into its envelope. I didn't dream, not once, but there was a soft darkness in which I hid from the night.

In the morning, the tree had tilted 45 degrees but it had not fallen.

Evil

A s I write this, I find myself remembering a conversation F and I had years before this happened. It's just
a snippet. I can't place the month or the year. I must have
been learning about heaven and hell in school. I must have
asked him a question. All I know is that he had made me
dinner – oven fries thick as my fingers. I was sliding them
into my mouth one by one. And he started to talk –

*You want to know about evil? Once when I was young
my parents had an exorcism. It wasn't a fun sort of exorcism. It was just the preacher, the new one. And my
parents, they had this brown leather couch and they made
me lie down on it. And close my eyes. I crossed my arms
over my chest.*

He made the gesture for a corpse. His hands cupped his
shoulders. I mimicked him, digging my nails into my
shoulder blades.

*That's right, Kitkat. I was trying to be funny, to make
my mom laugh. To admit they are being ridiculous. But
the ceiling fan is thwacking and this old guy is reading the
Bible over me. Verse after verse. For hours. His voice dron-
ing through his nose. And the couch smells rancid from
everything that has ever been dropped down the back.
And his voice goes on and on. And I'm hungry and I need
to pee. But the worst thing. The very worst thing. The*

thing I can't get away from is that my mother thinks I'm evil. She thinks I'm evil because I listen to the wrong kind of music, because I can't sleep, because I looked at my Dad wrong, because sometimes I get angry, because when my cousin shoved me for the hundredth time I broke his nose. Part of me wondered, I'd never have told them, but part of me wondered if they were right. If there was something rotten. I can't think of anything more evil. Nothing more fucking evil than making a child think they're evil. Never, Kit. Never ever let anyone make you feel like that. Remember this.

He sighed. *Then the guy got up and looked at me and my mother looked at me and I could see that they were all trying to tell if the evil was still there. And that they didn't fucking know.*

Did he know? It is too late to ask him. Do you know? I thought I had all of this straightened out in my mind. But sometimes if you've loved a person for a long time, it does not feel possible to slot them into Good and Evil so neatly. Not even if you think you should. And what would that mean for what I did? Could I really, looking back, say I was better than him?

3

I know it bothers you that I always slink back to my own place. I hate giving you flimsy apologies. I don't like to glance into the shadows at the imagined bodies of men as I pass through the city. I don't like the look I get at the corner shop when I buy a packet of cheesy crisps to eat as I walk. I want you to know that there is nothing I would like more than to wake up every day to the sound of you shuffling upright.

Maybe you'll think this is a longer version of the excuses people always make: I am like this or that because of my parents. I'm not trying to justify myself. But I thought you deserved to know.

Writing about the past has made me realise what a convincing adulthood I have constructed for myself. A job in which people thank me for my work, friends who text me on my birthday, some who sing. I've shared a house before, learnt to write in permanent marker on my bags of frozen bananas, squabbled about cleaning rotas. All that.

But when you asked about who came before you and I said *no one serious,* I think you believed I was joking or sparing your feelings. What I meant was that I had no compunctions about those people. I didn't care if I saw their faces slack with sleep or woke up to see them messaging their mothers. I suppose this makes me not a good person. I want to be better for you.

Last time you asked me to stay over, I almost did. You were so kind about my refusal afterwards – the way you walked me to the building's front door, the way you stood silhouetted against the night until I turned the corner. You even texted me, *Home safe?*

Safe.

Maybe I won't send this. Maybe I'll smile and say that I thought it over. That we should get a place together. I would give you a convincing rendition of adult-Katherine. Maybe that would be kinder?

A Shadow

Something dark had snaked through me. As I looked out my bedroom window, I noticed the tree angling its fragile hand towards the sky. I texted Andrew, hoping it might banish the feeling.

So bored . . . Tell me something fun.

He sent me a link to an article about the director of that butterfly-scientist TV show. I thought it was going to be a scandal. There were so many scandals at the time. But no, it was an interview in which he talked about driving through the desert into a storm of butterflies, how it felt like being inside of a kaleidoscope. Seeing all those fragile bodies survive the desert made him feel like perhaps there was hope for humanity after all. *Cool,* I texted back. And still that gummy feeling remained.

I walked to my parents' room where F still lay asleep, light from the edge of the window falling across his cheek. I looked at his shut eyes and the darts of stubble. Was he hurting M when we were asleep? We were not that sort of family. We were the sort of family who went on holiday to other old British towns and read from the metal plaques about the history of the cathedral or the fort or millworks. We were a family who picked up our sandwich wrappers when we left the train carriage.

When I was small, seven or eight, old enough to remember but barely, I walked in front of a car. We were all having lunch on some cafe's outdoor seating. Baby Leo was grizzling and I was bored. So, I got up and stepped off the pavement. Did I see something across the road? I don't know. Maybe it was a bird. Or a kazoo abandoned after someone's hen do. Something bright and tempting.

I didn't hear the car. I didn't see the car. I only felt F's chest knocking into me hard. My knees crashed into the paving. My body under his. My teeth slammed down on my tongue. And then he was holding me in the air and shaking me and shaking me. There was a sharpness to the pain in my neck. And maybe it was because I was crying or maybe because of the shaking, my vision went pink. And he was talking so loudly.

You could've died. You could've died. Never. Never. Do that.

How much can one moment change what you know of a person? I watched him sleep.

I went to brush my teeth. His wedding ring was sitting by the soap dish. The bar of soap was as twisted as driftwood and darkened with the mud of the previous day's work. I looked at the ring and thought about how adults walked around gilded like fancy teapots. Well, not Andrew's mum, who'd had him against his father's will and maintained Andrew was the best thing that had ever happened to her. But most of them. I picked the ring up. It was heavier than it looked and I put it on one hand. It was too big. I tried to clasp my hands together, as tight as I possibly could. Then I realised that I had been doing it wrong. They hadn't been palm to palm. His hand must have been pressing down around her fingers. I tried that and found that the metal barely registered, instead, it was the heat of compression. My fingers went the same red as M's. The knuckles of both the crushed and the crushing hands turned yellowish white.

What was I doing? All I had seen in my waking hours was F tugging M to the tree. His hand seeming too tight around hers. Would it have mattered if it wasn't for what I saw at night? But I'd caught her rushing to work that morning, a cherry dark blot on her lower lip, exactly where I'd seen it tear.

I couldn't tell M that my brain had been leaving my body. She'd look at me like I was a sick child, like nothing I knew to be true was true. I felt a cold current tugging and swirling through me, strong enough to pull the whole house underwater. And F – I didn't even know how to begin.

I slid the ring off and put it down. It clicked against the tiles.

Next to where the ring had been lying was his watch, the only thing he'd brought with him from his life in America. The face was pocked as the moon. On the back an engraving –

Days pass
as a shadow.
Ps. 144.4

The words were easy to read because years of dirt had darkened each letter. When I was young, I used to steal this watch and hold its ticking to my ear. The words were church words, the watch his own father's watch. Stolen or given, I never knew. The watch strap was old, the leather mottled, and more than one hole had been stretched by the buckle. I looked at the gold of the ring and the gold of the watch. F would notice if either went missing. And yet, I wanted them both. I wanted something familiar to carry with me. Something sturdier than a fleeting impression, words overheard, and replayed until I didn't trust them. As if a relic of the family I'd believed I'd had might ward off the possibility of seeing anything worse. That want was ocean-cold and filled me entirely. It told me I deserved it, that I could take it, that it would be easy.

I wrapped my fist around the watch. It felt solid and reassuring, as a father's watch should. And then M was shouting my name from downstairs and I was shouting back to ask what she wanted. She'd decided we should go shopping as this was the last Saturday on which she would be free.

I took the watch with me in my jacket. The denim was thick and I was sure that no one could see the watch from the outside, but I could feel the steady pull of it holding me down. There were few shops in our town: an Oxfam, the Sainsbury's, places for tourists to buy patterned smocks and necklaces made of sea glass. So, we drove up to the bigger town where M worked. M did not listen to music when she drove. And the windows blocked out the sound of the sea. The loudest noise was Leo's phone in the back making the sounds of exploding spaceships. *Kssssssshhh-pow.*

You didn't like the tree. I opened the glove compartment to look inside. There was only a repair manual and a single toffee in clear plastic. It crinkled loudly as I unwrapped it. I put it in my mouth feeling the dust fleck-ing my tongue.

What makes you say that? M turned onto the roundabout.

You didn't say anything.

I was remembering.

Remembering what? Leo piped up from the back.

I fingered the watch. The sides were ridged as if by minutes.

Nothing much. M kept her eyes on the road

What's with yellow plums? I asked.

She took one hand off the steering wheel to tuck her hair behind her ear.

Look at the phone will you – is the construction still going on the A road?

It was. Yellow plums were a ridiculous thing to have a secret about. And then she said, *When I met your father . . .*

Leo interrupted, *In America!*

We both knew that it was M who had rescued F from his small town. She had been driving through on a road trip and stopped for pie and what the Americans called gas. He'd been working behind the pie counter. And when he saw her he'd fallen in love, or so the story went. He'd got to chatting with her and then asked to hitch a ride. He'd followed her right out of the yellow clapboard cafe and into her car and stayed with her ever since. It was a good story. I liked to imagine my mother as the stranger driving into town, her eyes full of the biggest sky she'd ever seen, stealing a local boy. But I couldn't imagine my mother letting a strange man into her car.

M looked over at her golden child and it seemed as if she might stop talking. But then she began again. *About a hundred miles out of town, when it was getting dark, I told your father that I needed to sleep. And that he could sleep on the side of the road or that I could drop him off in a motel. But I wasn't sharing the car with him.*

Why? Leo asked.

Grown-ups don't like to share rooms or, I suppose, cars with people they don't know very well. And anyway, I went to sleep on the back seat, which wasn't comfortable. But I was stretching my savings, only stopping at a motel every three days to shower. I had a blanket. And then I woke up and your father was hitting the window with his fist. I thought something had gone wrong. I wound down the glass. He was trying to persuade me to let him inside the car. And Kit, let this be a warning to you.

That if I meet strange men, I'll marry them? I couldn't stop myself. She always spoke to me as if I was about to misstep.

Don't be a teenager.

I am a teenager.

Anyway, I told him no. And he told me there were snakes in America and I told him he should have thought of that before volunteering to drive with me to California. He kept knocking. I closed my eyes and pulled the blanket over my head and waited for him to go away. I decided that in the morning, I would leave him there by the road and he could get a ride from somebody else.

I looked out at the scrubby green land and hedges we were driving by. I had never seen a hitchhiker, although sometimes we passed families in shiny cagoules, lined up like ducks.

So I woke up and folded my blanket and climbed over the gearshift to the front seat. He was curled up, sleeping on the nose of the car. I beeped.

Leo imitated the noise of a car horn. It was a noise he still loved though we had told him enough times that honking was illegal unless there was an emergency.

And your father, he wakes up and stands. His hair is every which way. And I'm about to drive off when I see he's moving, slowly and strangely, and when he turns around his arms are full of all these yellow plums. Apparently in the night he couldn't sleep so he just started walking and he stole them from someone's garden. And he's holding them out to me and it's clear he's offering them. And he looks so proud of himself and so sweet that I let him back in. We ate those plums all the way across the state line.

After that Leo wanted to know what a plum tasted like and we told him that he knew and he said he couldn't remember. You have younger siblings, you know how this goes. I put my fingers around the watch and felt it ticking.

I had not known the story of the yellow plums, but I knew what came next. What came next was me. It was one of those family stories, I can remember it told in F's voice and then M's with their individual quirks. I guess I'll tell you it in mine.

What happened next was that F was still in love with my mother, with the beautiful girl who swept him out of his town like a rushing river. And M was still ambivalent, unsure if she wanted to keep carrying this twig-like man along with her. M began to suspect that something was going on inside of herself around the time they reached San Francisco. Her body had always been quite regular, quite well behaved and it had gone off-kilter. She took the test and wondered whether to tell F. She thought that if her child had his height, or his wide smile it would be no bad thing. But to get that from a father you needed only a squirt of genetics. Her boyfriends before that point had been of the casual kind, men who made her laugh. Close enough that she fell asleep beside them riding home on the bus after meeting their friends at the pub. But not people with whom she shared plans. F looked at her like he was trying to create an Ordnance Survey map of her peaks and curves and points of interest, which both flattered her and made her feel unsure. She did tell him in the end. She had decided she wanted the baby and she wanted it to have a chance to know its father. But she told herself this was a probation. She was prepared to go it alone.

Her love for him grew slowly. As I grew feet and ankles and toes, my invisible twin was love. He cooked her meals, the cherry pie that she craved, but also spinach soup to feed my unfurling brain. He talked to me through her stomach. He told me stories about angels and saints. Stories of the Nephilim, the gigantic children of fallen angels and human women. Stories of Uriel, who denounced the fallen angels. Saraqâêl, the archangel who judges those who sin in the spirit. M told him she didn't need a child who was afraid of God. She didn't believe and until then had only known those who thought of God as a sweeping

100

benevolence. F had grown up with people who believed not just in the Bible that M had seen in each motel drawer but in other books, narrow well-thumbed books, that spoke of fires and angels. He told her that he didn't know what was true but that these were his version of *The Three Bears* and *Little Red Riding Hood*. They were weird stories for a baby, but F's tone was one of love. Apparently, I would kick up each time I heard his voice, as if saying *Hello. Hello.*

She married him in a registry office in Norwich, the town where she'd studied. Charlie was there. And some of her other university friends. She was worried F had no one but he only smiled and said that he had me, the best baby.

In the shopping centre, she bought me a new coral red backpack and brown suede boots that she made me promise not to wear on the beach because they would be ruined. She forbade me one dress because it was too short but agreed that I could have some glow-in-the-dark shoelaces. Leo wanted some new Lego but she told him *no* and only bought him new wellies. Then it was time to do the food shop.

On the way home, M told us not to talk because she had a headache.

Outside the house as we were lifting out the bags, she said, *I hope you like your new stuff.*

And I nodded because I had chosen them.

It might be the last time for a while, she said.

I know. Saturdays.

No. I mean, you're old enough to know. We're going to have to be careful with money for a bit.

101

Leo said, *Why?* And we both turned to look at him. He played with the edge of his T-shirt.

Never mind. Remember, Kit, don't wear the boots on the beach. Okay?

Watching

W*e're home! We're home!* Leo shouted as we came in through the door.

F was at the kitchen table bent over his laptop. Our house had two bedrooms, one bathroom, a kitchen, a TV room, and a narrow room truncated by the bend in the stairs. This room had one small window and was what F called his study. It was filled with second-hand office filing cabinets that were stuffed with LPs, cassettes, bent-backed novels, bills, an old monitor and a laptop that was broken but which he wouldn't throw out for fear of data thieves. Too many things. This meant that more often than not he worked in the kitchen.

The screen flowed with the secret language of computers. Code was something I thought I should understand but didn't.

Leo, he said.

Mmm? Leo, who had avoided taking in any bags, was already deep inside the world of his game. That he could play and walk and avoid furniture was a gift.

What have I told you about touching my things? F asked.

I didn't.

You didn't what?

I didn't.

103

How do you know what you didn't do if I haven't even told you what it is?

But I didn't.

M started telling me to unpack the groceries. Soba, udon and furikake from the Asian Mart near the shopping centre went in the top cupboard for dry goods, while frozen peas and those dinosaur turkey nuggets Leo liked had to be scooted into the freezer. She handed Leo the frozen things because they were to be stored at his height.

I'm talking to my son, F said.

Well, you can talk to him while he puts this away.

I didn't, Leo said.

He's taken my watch, F said.

I stood on a chair to slot in the noodles and rice. There was so much noise in the kitchen that I knew no one could hear the watch in my pocket.

I didn't. I didn't. I didn't.

Maybe you put it down, said M. *Have you checked under the bed, or in your pockets? Leo: Nuggets. Freezer. Or do you want them to defrost?*

Leo stood clutching the bag of nuggets and his game to his chest, arms crossed.

Where did you last have it? M asked.

I'd stored the noodles, and knew that I should cut across the kitchen for carrots and broccoli and onions. *Maybe we left it in the garden,* I said.

F shut his computer. *You shouldn't take what isn't yours.*

I didn't. Leo began to snivel. Not to cry exactly but to scrunch up his face like an old tissue. Water dripped from the bag of nuggets onto the floor.

If you give it back to me by tomorrow—

Don't bully him. M had put herself between F and Leo.

The watch fattened my pocket. It was too late to give it back. My brother protested with such childish righteousness that surely he'd be believed.

I ran the pad of my thumb over the engraving – the quote from his holy book. F always said that God was everywhere in the town he grew up in. I thought of God in my pocket watching the scene. Well, he should have put higher fences around his apple tree, if he'd wanted better behaviour. Anyway, I didn't give the watch back, which may or may not have affected what happened that night. I long for omniscience, to be one of those writers able to dip in and out of the heads of other people. But even now I can only line up the events.

Leo go put your new wellies in your room. M flicked her wrist to dismiss him. *Gabriel, we can talk about this later, can't we?*

Leo seemed momentarily confused, looking down at the nuggets in his hand.

Give those here. I stepped off the chair and took them from Leo. The cold packet felt good against my hot palm. F didn't say anything.

When I woke next to my body, I wanted to crawl into it again. To pretend that nothing was happening. But I heard a sound and I felt my body shift uneasily beside me. It was only a small sound. A gasp. Or a cough. Fairly quiet. The sort of sound you lie there willing to come again so you can dismiss it. But it didn't. Only the persistent wind. And

I couldn't relax into the body which was meanwhile moving, shuffling.

I walked to the landing. I heard the sound again. It was a strange noise, almost a cough. The sort of cough you make when a particle of food has lodged in your throat. It died back. Stopped. Then it appeared again.

Fight or flight – that's what adrenaline is supposed to make you do. You leap forward or leap back. I accept that. What I don't understand is the choice between the two, how do you know if you will beat back the wolves or outpace them? I've always been a flyer. You know that. I'd already fled from my own body. But in the hallway, a synapse took a different path and I hurried toward the coughing.

In a house where the doors were always open, I'd always taken my parents' shut door to mean romantic intimacies I wouldn't want to witness. I touched the wood and felt the grain through the paint. The walls in that house were thin and built by hands long buried. Now the sound was really quite loud. I'd never opened their shut door. But I walked through it. I couldn't not.

They were having sex. F was on top of M and he was holding her down by the throat. His forearms balanced on her shoulders, his elbows digging into the pillow. M's eyes were shut but her mouth was open. Hiccups of air escaped. M and F were both partway dressed. M's shirt buttons caught the light of the bedside lamp as they bounced up and down. F's boxer shorts were caught around his ankles. They were red with Christmas trees on.

The flashes of flesh felt at once strange and familiar. I still remembered the way they had bathed with me ten years or so before. I'd scrubbed both their backs. M had liked me to scratch hers and I'd liked seeing the way the pressure of my nails turned her skin moon-white. I'd seen F's body too. I was young enough to remember and old enough to cringe at the way I'd pressed my thumb into the pink studs of his nipples and called them buttons. I'd peered into the dark cavity of his ears.

Even after everything else I'd witnessed, none of this meant I wanted to watch them fuck. The lights were on and I could see them clearly. I knew I should leave. Teenagers walk in on their parents and then they walk out. But his hands were on her throat. I told myself that as soon as he lifted them, I would leave, as soon as I could tell myself that everything was fine.

I focused on the muscle between M's eyebrows. The flesh pushed into a cherry-pit lump. Pain? Concentration? Pleasure? I looked for M's hands searching for a gesture that might tell me how she was feeling. One was hidden by sheets but the other unresisting flat on the bed. She was wearing a thin gold bangle and her own watch. Unlike F's it was new and black plastic. M had explained that she wore it because it made it easy to check the time without a patient noticing and feeling disrupted. F's hand around M's neck appeared larger than in daily life. M's head was tilted up. I reached in my pyjama pocket, fumbling for a ghostly version of the watch and its ridges but then I remembered that it was ticking under my pillow.

M lay there. I knew the words – *Bondage, Dominance, Sadomasochism*. Was that what this was? I knew them the same way I knew *sex-positive* and *slut shaming* and *consent*. I believed that what consenting adults did was their own business. I still do. But then the belief was still academic. No one had ever pinned me under them. The bed shifted with F's motion. M turned her head to the side. F lifted one hand off M's neck and balanced it on the wall. M didn't struggle, but the remaining hand still looked heavy.

It was the same bed that Leo and I got into at Christmas. It was the place we opened stockings together. Leo's new crayons had spilt over the sheets leaving purple, pink and green marks that M correctly predicted would never come off. F had said people would pay good money for such artistic sheets. Stuck to the fridge, there was a photograph of Leo and me lying on our backs next to the marks.

I watched the two bodies in the bed, at once trying to see them and trying to unsee them. I thought of how that same Christmas, Leo got bored of putting up decorations, pleading that the needles of the tree hurt. M explained that you had to be sure to brush the needles the right way. Replaying this in my head, it sounded like a warning. But it might not have been.

I looked back to the hand that remained on her neck. The thumb didn't quite press down on the hollow of her neck but to the side. His nails were cut down to the pink for the guitar. I comforted myself that it would not scratch. His toes were tucked under him and I thought of my own toes on the white plastic starting block of the swimming pool.

Images thudded through my head, competing with the scene in front of me. Had I been created in this tight grip? I hadn't thought of it before, never pictured the details.

You wouldn't, would you? You don't want to ask yourself did your mother have a good time? Was it quiet? Was it loud? M closed her eyes, going completely still like a frog playing dead.

And then it was done. M touched his arm, got out of bed, took her phone from the bedside table and walked to the bathroom. F was quickly up again, humming. I heard him knock on the bathroom door and ask M if she wanted tea. M said she was *fine*. Again, I wondered if I had got something wrong. If I had misunderstood. If the things I had barely seen were a secret code between the two people I knew best.

The toilet flushed but I didn't hear M's feet. I went to her. I suppose because I was scared and I wanted my mother. Or perhaps, it was nothing so innocent. Perhaps I was angry at everything she had kept from me. Or at the way that she had let herself be grasped like that.

Walking through doors had begun to feel easy. Simple. It was a slit of darkness inside the wood and then out again. Our bathroom was small. Door, sink, loo and bath huddled together. M was standing in front of the sink. She touched her neck in the places that F's hands had been. The only place for me to stand was right by her shoulder. My height had just outstripped hers and it still gave me a hazy vertigo to be taller than my mother. There was no mark.

I thought again of F's hand over her shoulder, around her hand, on her neck. Was he trying to pin her down? To catch her before she went to some secret place in her own head? It was not until later that I learnt how fear can fix you silent and rigid. Not until years more, that I realised

109

that I too often go somewhere hidden in my own mind, that sometimes it is all you can do.

I wanted to touch her then. To put my hands where his had been, to feel what he had felt. And I did.

Her neck was warm. The skin was skin. Same as mine. Same as Leo's. Or different. But not so different. I'm trying to tell you all of this in such a straightforward way. As if you were there standing right by me, holding my hand. And I admit sometimes, I'm unsure. I can't remember what her skin felt like that night. I can't summon that, so I say it felt like skin. Skin like mine. Writing this to you, I keep touching my own neck and thumbing the ridge of my collar bone. Can you imagine your own mother holding you? It won't be anything like that night. Still, if you can summon it up, then why not let yourself be held?

I didn't touch her neck for long. She turned from me and cranked the shower on. She placed her phone by the soap. She began to quickly unbutton down to her black sports bra. M didn't believe in lace or underwires. There were bruises on her right shoulder. They must have been older than this night, because there were no marks on her neck. From that first night with the Marigold glove? I tried to remember which side he'd been standing on and found that I could move my looming father like a paper doll. Left? Right? The bruises were the size of thumbprints or the size of the sliver of soap on the sink or the size of new school erasers, pink and dark and small. I tried to feel good about the smallness. I knew that some people liked it rough. I'd heard the boys say it. She likes it rough. People did. There was a feeling when I was swimming laps when I'd gone too long in the water, when the pain was not in my arms or my legs but filling even my lungs which was good. It felt like being sharpened. I felt strong because I could hold all that pain and keep going.

M leant closer to the mirror as if checking for wrinkles. I tried to think if water sounded different hitting a body and if F downstairs could know that no one was washing. M's expression was steady. It was as if even here in the secrecy of the bathroom she was keeping things from me.

M picked up the phone and began to photograph her shoulders, left and then right. She was using the better of the phone's two cameras, facing the screen towards the bathroom mirror. In the reflection I could see the smaller photographed M. I recognised the pose. I had taken secret bathroom photographs of myself. I never sent them to anyone, they were mine alone. But I wanted to keep track of myself. I wondered if that was why M was taking these photos? Or if they were for someone else.

I imagined talking to F through bullet-proof glass and the sound of his singing coming through a prison's telephone. I saw myself standing up in court, asked to testify what I had seen, what I had known. I wondered, could I stand there and say he had done it? Or would I tell them that in sixteen years, he had only been kind? Strange. Perhaps in some families they did not play the boat game, but instead the murder game. Whose side would you take? Who would you testify for?

M wedged her phone behind the cold tap and began to brush her teeth. The electric toothbrush hummed insistently. M spat and splashed her face with warm water. The quiet felt obscene. Things like this were supposed to be loud. Not small and silent and happening in my bathroom.

She took off the rest of her clothes and got into the shower. I stayed because part of me still believed the night would spit up an answer. I stayed as she soaped and bubbled. I stayed until my mother walked right through me.

Other Families

The next night there was a party and I decided it would be good to be out of the house. It might unfog my brain. M came into my room as I was getting ready. I was wearing a dress I'd got second-hand months before but never had a chance to wear. It was silver with a thick industrial zipper that ran all the way from the hem to my collar bone – it made me think of a body bag but in a nice way.

You're going out like that? M asked. The phrase heavy and unoriginal as if she were reading from some motherhood script.

So? In the past I would have said more. But I didn't have the energy to fight her, so I went back to trying to make the fiddly catch on my necklace work.

They're going to want to unzip you. She picked Leo's Lego bricks off the floor one by one and dropped them click, click in their box.

They? I thought of Andrew unzipping it carefully the same way he did with the little blue plastic wallet in which he kept his good fineliners.

Do you know what objectified means?

I didn't bother replying to that.

It means being turned into a thing. Some of the girls who come to my sessions – that's what they want.

x

113

People think these girls dress like they do because they are stupid. But they're not. They're scared of being people. People have responsibilities. If you're an object, no one can blame you for anything. So these girls do everything they can to make themselves into objects. But they don't realise that if they do that someone's going to pick them up and carry them somewhere they don't want to go.

I undid the top of the zip a centimetre so that it looked like a crocodile with its mouth slightly open.

I thought you believed in women wearing what they want?

I do. There were no more Lego bricks studding the carpet and we were both still for a moment listening to the sound of Leo's cartoons rising up the stairs.

Do the girls ever ask you if you're happy, M? Like, they've come to see you in that room with the brown carpet so you can unobject them or something? Do they ask you if you're happy?

Sometimes, she said.

What do you say? This came out soft. I could feel myself willing something from her. Some definitive statement that she had chosen this. I'm embarrassed. How could that have been what I wanted? But it was. I wanted her to pat my shoulder and to tell me that everything was under control.

I say it's not their job to worry about my happiness. It's my job to worry about theirs. And she leant over and pulled up the crocodile zip, her knuckles grazing my throat.

Text me when you're on your way home, she said.

Years before, she'd broken her arm falling down the stairs. I was at swimming practice but she told me that she'd tripped on our toys, her body skidding out from under her. She'd let me and Leo draw all over the cast. He was so young that his marks were a green haze of scribble. I'd done a long line of cats. Red and orange and blue cats with thick stiff whiskers. She had healed completely and it was probably unrelated to anything I'd seen. As she walked away, I watched her arm as if the bone itself might testify. I wanted to be drunk.

The party was at Lia's. I know you don't know Lia. She hasn't been introduced. I didn't know her that well myself. Her name was like another name with the beginning lopped off – *Amelia, Cordelia, Cecilia* – but teachers taking register always read it out with the same sigh they held for the rest of us and never offered a longer version.

She annoyed me. Whenever anyone was scrolling on their phone she used to lean over, slotting her head close to her victim's, and ask *What are you looking at?* She'd done it to Andrew once or twice and he was always looking at some monster and she'd say, *Weeeeeeeiiiirrrrrrddddddddddddd.* Or she'd ask questions in a slow babyish voice. *Is that how you want to dress, Andrew? Is that how you want your girl-friend to dress, oh sorry, your boyfriend? With wings? Is that what you like?* He would stand very still and wait for her to flit off as if she were a large wasp.

I wasn't a particular focus of hers. She had a riff that I'd seen her in town and hadn't waved. She kept asking, *Kit, why were you ignoring me?* Until I said, *Because I felt like*

115

it, Lia. Though I'd never seen her. Her face fell in on itself and then exploded outwards in a slightly manic laughter.

In another school her opinion might have mattered more but our school had no royalty. Our social lives were more like those of the gulls. No particular leaders but sometimes the whole class would swoop together as a group on Miss Ellis who taught Double Science. Someone would start talking and then we all would begin whooping, our voices rising upwards, and someone would turn on a Bunsen burner. Someone else would start slowly burning the ends of their hair, watching the strands grey and curl. Until Miss Ellis was crying.

But also, we had fun. Shimmery, drunk, a little high, full of music and speculation. We could be kind to each other then. The unmemorable stories we told each other and half heard were a kind of drug all by themselves, the way they wove us together.

None of my friends had house parties, our homes were liable to have parents in them. We had the park and the beach and, worst case, the arcades where we could usually loiter for a few hours before we were kicked out. But Lia's place was the exception.

Lia lived in the biggest house I'd been inside, windows taller than me and that plaster stuff up by the ceiling shaped into bunches of grapes. But lots of those windows didn't open and plants poked their heads up from her drains and weird stains ran down the walls.

Her mum was always asleep upstairs or wandering through the kitchen with a benign and hazy expression. We guessed that Lia's dad had left years ago, because her mum was like this, or that his leaving had done it. She

116

looked like a more rumpled Lia. Their eyes were the same colour, a washed-out blue, but Lia's mum's always seemed out of focus as if she were missing her prescription. Still, the expression in her eyes implied she saw a nice sort of blur.

Andrew was supposed to meet me there. He always came to Lia's parties. His face was too symmetrical for any of the things she said about him to gather energy. There were already people lying on the sofa and watching TV. I looked around for him and spotted the usual suspects: the beers in shopping bags; the boy in the middle of the carpet making everyone's roll ups; the islands of people clustered together; the couple with their tongues in each other's mouths, pink proboscises flashing in and out. I felt the silver snake of the zipper press down my centre line.

Flashes of the night before arrived like emails I could not unsubscribe from. I wanted Andrew – the steadiness of him. The way he would weave a story around my head. Being with Andrew was my favourite thing about being at parties. We never spent the whole night together, we had other friends – a loose collection of bodies whose names I have never told you. But he was like a ladder at the deep end of the pool. I knew I could get myself out with my arms alone. But he meant I never had to.

Where are you? I texted him.

A friend came over and I complimented her outfit which was genuinely good. She'd started plucking her eyebrows and it had changed her face. She looked more focused now. She asked me how I thought I'd done on my exams and I shrugged. *Don't make that face,* she said. *You always do well.*

What can I say? I'm a genius.

She rolled her eyes. I asked her how anal had gone. We knew things about each other in those days. Strange intimate things. I suppose it was easier to talk about our bodies because they still felt like borrowed costumes. I knew that her boyfriend had been pressuring her to try.

Hurt like a bitch.

Did you like it?

She looked dramatically over her shoulder left and right before saying. *Not as bad as I thought.*

I wanted to ask her if that meant good? Or something else?

Lia's mum came down. She was wearing a T-shirt with Bugs Bunny on it, his face stretched across her breasts. I used to wonder if it was living by the sea that did it. If the sort of adults who wanted to be on a beach vacation forever weren't real adults. Later I decided adulthood was a mirage, forever moving away from you.

Tea? she asked, not seeming to notice that we were both drinking vodka out of little paper cups. The taste of the alcohol was almost cleansing.

Okay, I said. *Thanks.*

My friend rolled her eyes. Lia's mum got down a mug with a fat yellow chick on it.

I wanted Andrew and also, absurdly, I wanted to hug Lia's mum. She put three white teaspoons of sugar in the mug without asking. *You girls having fun?* she asked.

Mm-hmm, I said.

I'm glad Lia has such good friends.

118

Lia's great, I lied.

It's safer isn't it? You all being here and not on the streets.

Thank you for having us.

You're very welcome, she said. She paused, looking at me in her hazy way, and then she licked the pad of her thumb and pressed it to my face. Her finger was wet and hard.

You had a bit of something, mascara.

Thank you, I said again.

My friend made an aghast face and, after Lia's mum wandered off, I asked, *Have you seen Andrew?*

She shook her head. The party was a sprawling thing and I wandered from place to place with my paper cup of vodka, looking down into its purity. It smelt of almost nothing. And my face was hot. I was a good drinker then, better than I am now in some ways. But normally I drank slowly and that night I found myself chasing the ethanol-lift.

People split off in usual and unusual pairings. I saw a girl I knew passed out on the sofa. Her head angled as if she were staring into the ceiling. Next to her was a boy who we'd all made fun of a few years before for the way he farted in class, *Parp, parp, parp.* We called him Lord Fartington, with such wit and invention. He had his hand down her shirt and was moving it along her breasts.

A thought formed that I should stop him. The thought hung there suspended in the vodka and I realised I was sitting down. And a fear came over me and I thought of what M had said about the zipper and of being unzipped in the middle of the room on the strange carpet.

Then Lia was next to me.

Where's Andrew? she asked. And for a moment I stared at her mouth, shiny with gloss replaying its motions to be sure she had said it and not me.

Dunno.

I don't understand why you two are so secretive.

Not.

Are you sure?

Ysss.

I looked at her birdy face and wondered if she'd put something in my drink. I didn't normally feel like this. But it had been pure. *Pure,* I thought and I giggled thinking of nuns and American girls on television.

Well, if you aren't using him. Maybe I'll have a go.

What?

It's environmentally right. Waste not. Want not.

You hate him.

No, I don't. And then I had to recast Lia as a different person. As a person who really wanted to know what was happening in Andrew's life. Who really wanted to know what it was that he liked. I wished people would stop slipping out of their roles like bad actors determined to add their own spin on their characters. Only I didn't think it so clearly.

Stay, I said to Lia. *Going home.* If I didn't say too many words, she wouldn't hear the wobble in my voice.

As I got up, I saw that Lord Fartington had buried his face in the girl's neck. I tilted my way home and back to bed and by the time I was at my front door sentences had returned to my brain. If not sober, I was no longer lost in brain mist. I slipped inside past the sound of F's record player and tiptoed upstairs and landed straight on my bed ready to puddle into sleep. Just then a text lit up my phone. *Sry distracted. See you there?*

I tried to move to text him – or I thought I did – but a thick darkness covered me for a while. And when my hand reached forwards for the phone it was only my sleep-hand. I'd been subject to that margin of not-sleep not-awake whose exact duration I never understood. I got up and hurried through the night, once taking a shortcut through someone's dark kitchen and once through a garden heady with white flowers.

By the time I got back, the living room was littered with bodies in natural and pharmaceutical sleep. Andrew wasn't there. Lia's mum was stooping to gather paper cups. Lord Fartington had disappeared. And that girl still lay passed out.

I stopped writing this to search for that unconscious girl online. And from what I saw she seems to be happy now. She's smiling wide and her hair looks soft and clean. I want to believe she's fine.

My tea was on the countertop and I remembered that I hadn't drunk it. Lia's mum poured it out. No one stirred at its splashing sound. I hope she didn't remember making it for me. I should have drunk that tea.

I followed her upstairs to Lia's room. Lia's room was pink. Pink fluffy pillow and a vase of dried roses tied with a blue ribbon. You could almost ignore that the wallpaper was peeling.

Lia's mum – I had no other name for her – approached the bed where Lia slept. In sleep Lia looked less avian and more rodent, like a rabbit even. F had once told me that his father shot rabbits and hung them up by their ears. But Lia did not look hung up. She looked well rested, healthy even.

Lia's mum pulled the covers up gently over her daughter.

Insomniac Hours

Andrew told me that he'd never gone to the party. When I didn't reply, he assumed I'd already left. Over the next few weeks, there were other parties in other locations. I went to some of them and so did he. I met the other girls on the swim team for a few lazy practices that culminated in beers and takeaways. But certain thoughts lapped at my days. F on top of M. M in the mirror. If there was nowhere to go, I kept my body awake with dance music pumped in through my headphones and videos of minimalists throwing their lives away item by item. It wasn't hard to stay up. My body, as if not wanting to be abandoned, had become jittery. Unable to settle.

I'd wait for Leo to fall asleep. The moment was hard to detect – he was a twitchy sleeper. His fingers moved as if he was tickling the side of a dog I couldn't see. Then, I'd go downstairs. Usually F would already be alone, M asleep or at least in their bedroom.

There's something you need to understand – I loved him. Not in some Freudian way, not as a deep subconscious secret. No, F had sliced my carrots small. F had taught me how to sing, looked into my eyes and repeated each note, again and again. Even now, people are surprised by how well I carry a tune. He was the person who used to cut my hair at the kitchen table and who showed me that he was keeping some in a paper envelope in case I wanted it when I was older – for memorabilia or to make a locket of my own hair. F loved me. He wasn't some monster from the sea. He was my father.

I was sure nothing too bad could happen if he knew I was there. He sat in his chair with his small drink and a little notebook – the kind you can buy in any old shop, with a spiral top and thin pages, that smell a little like classrooms. He'd be writing words, lyrics. His handwriting was not joined up but it was very ordered, almost like type.

I asked him questions. They were the sort of questions that I had asked when I was Leo's age and was trying to find a guidebook to being alive. Part of me thought that maybe if I asked enough questions, he'd explain what was going on. Wasn't that how M's job worked? You ask enough open-ended questions and people will tell you their truths.

We'd sit side by side in the warm kitchen light and he seemed happy to answer. In the same way that he'd been happy to answer my childhood questions of *Where does the rain come from?* or *Why are there seven days in a week?*

Question 1: *What age were you happiest?*

When he sang in the church choir. It wasn't Catholic, so no uniforms. A guy with a tambourine and another with an acoustic guitar. He could have sung there forever. They would have forgiven his voice for breaking. They didn't ask for purity, only enthusiasm. But one day he didn't believe in their God anymore and he had to find a new music.

Or maybe, he said, *it was when you were born. Maybe then, because even though people say it is terrible that babies don't sleep, it was as if my body was made for it, as if I'd evolved specially to stay up late holding a new creature.*

Question 2: *How did you know M was the one?*

Seeing her was like seeing home or seeing the future. *Shitty men are attracted to weak women,* he said. M was so strong that you could tie a hurricane to her and it would hold still. When he saw her, he understood why Dante's spirit guide had not been a saint or a philosopher but a girl he had loved.

Question 3: *Why didn't you try to become a singer? Professionally, I mean.*

He didn't come from the sort of people who tell you that you can be anything. He came from the sort of people who thought you'd be lucky to hold onto this earth a little longer. Leaving them had taken all his energy.

Question 4: *Do you regret coming to this town?*

He had never been attached to places, only people. And he had us here.

Question 5: *Are you happy now?*

Talking to you, Caterpillar? Yes.

Question 6: *What are you most afraid of?*

Losing his family. When asked to elaborate on this, to give a circumstance, he said, *In any way.*

Question 6.5 – *Even more afraid of that than of going deaf?*

Yes. Even more than going deaf. Because he would keep all the songs in his head. Beethoven had. But a child is a song that keeps changing.

Question 7 – *Is there something you wish for?*

His preacher used to speak of angels. Spirals of light or winged lions with eyes all over their feathers. When he was a child, F had wanted to see these angels more than he'd wanted to see God or the man with holes in his hands. The preacher told him there was an angel for snow and one for rain, one for thunder, one for wind. They each had names and F wrote them out in fine pencil under his bedroom windowsill, where he could see them each time he lay down. He loved Metatron best who had 72 wings and who sat with God. But then, when F was seven or nine, there was a shift in the leaders. Some holy politics above his head. The old man had retired and the new preacher did not care for angels. He said that the true holy book had little to say on angels. But still F had wanted to see angels. He'd wanted to see something burning with holy fire. But no angels appeared.

I might be combining his answers with those he'd given on other days. They say that each time you recall a memory, you change it. And I have recalled these too many times to count. At first, I was still playing the boat game, and later after I'd made the wrong choice and it was too late.

I didn't say – *Did you change? Is this you?*

Those aren't questions people actually ask each other. But I wish I had. I miss him. Despite everything, I miss him. Sometimes I ask these questions in my head. Sometimes he replies. But I know these are answers I've made up. Sometimes I only get the echoing of my own skull.

One night, he showed me how to mend a tear in a shirt.

The shirt in question was his soft sage cotton shirt – the shirt he had worn to every Sun Songs since we arrived in the town. There was a pinprick-hole in the back. He talked as he threaded up and over the gap, describing each stitch, *Over and over and one more time over, then knot, careful not to catch the needle. Almost done. Look at this ridge, you've got to massage it out.* His hands moved over the cotton, gentle and innocuous.

There was no break from wondering. There was no moment when I might escape into another world, a dream body, meet new monsters. There was no moment that I could ever slip out of my life. In or out of my body, it didn't matter. I was trapped in that town, trapped with F and M and Leo. I considered hopping on the late train to the city. But what escape was that? I would still be thinking of them. Thought with no end.

It was one of those nights, chasing the same loop of thoughts that I decided to finally have sex with Andrew.

Donkey-Men

On museum days, I left the house as early as I could, happy to have a place to go. But sometimes this meant that I had to wait outside until Cassandra arrived. She had the only key. I usually texted Andrew while I waited.

That day I wrote, *Meet in the allotments tonight?* I had walked past them during a night-self walk, noted the tiny sheds clustered together like an elf-village and the low hop-able fence. It would be a good place to be unseen.

Time? he wrote. I smiled, because it was time, wasn't it? To learn what it meant to break into each other. To learn pain and pleasure.

9?

I stood against the cool wall. Pasted to the window there was an advert for the Sun Songs two years ago. F had played then too. The flyer had faded. Everything decays faster by the sea. Windows need to be replaced more often. The salt eats the frames. It nibbles paint. The sun swallows colour from flags and signs. Tourists find this cute. But the way the moon and the sun and the sea were conspiring to erase our efforts at civilisation made me uneasy. Anyway, F's name was still visible in small black font. I was reading it and wondering if this had always been going on, even then. Even when he stood on stage and said, *This one is for a Caterpillar I know* and I'd tried to hide behind a plastic cup of lemonade.

I wondered if I should ask Cassandra if we could put up a new poster. Did Cassandra worry about her parents?

The watch was in my left pocket because I couldn't think of anywhere safe to leave it at home. In the other pocket was my only condom. We had each been given them to put on courgettes in PSHE. The vegetables all looked diseased, the green speckles visible through the latex. Afterwards they'd handed out extras. Some of the boys had grabbed fistfuls.

The circular face of the watch and the circle of the condom were almost identical in size. I took the watch out and it told me that it was five minutes past the hour. But then I heard Cassandra shouting my name.

Sorry, I'm late. Drama with my sister.

Drama?

Yeah, she lives out in Cornwall with her husband. Anyway, they've been fighting.

I nodded like I knew what it meant for a sister to call me about her husband. I couldn't imagine Leo with a wife.

Well, he's taken her wedding rings and buried them in the garden. But he won't tell her where. And she won't listen to me. She's going crazy about it. But if they don't stay married what does she need the rings for anyway? She unlocked the door. *But that's my sister for you.*

Do you have a—?

Girlfriend's in London.

Cool. Nice.

Cassandra got out her phone and showed me a picture of a smiling woman wearing a beanie and holding a paper coffee cup. I was surprised, because she seemed so not alternative, so un-Cassandra. She looked like one of those women in stock photos.

You'll meet her when she comes down to visit. Tea? We had an electric kettle we kept in the bottom desk drawer.

I'm good.

Cassandra hefted out an old cardboard box. Cardboard around here got soft. It wasn't wet or even damp and yet you had a sense that water was dissolving it at a rate too slow for the human eye. She opened it up to show me photographs. The photos were postcard-size and faded, yellowed at the edges. All were of donkeys.

Found it at the back of the cupboard. Someone must have been going to put together an exhibit on the beach donkeys. Anyway, I thought it could be fun for families, maybe a display around Christmas – tie it into the whole Mary thing, but you know, not too religious. Go through and find the ones with the sweetest faces, can you?

This was harder than it sounded. The donkeys' faces were donkey faces, sweet of course, but all donkeys are kind of the same. Big eyes and long ears.

It was the children, splay-legged over the backs of the animals that interested me. A young girl, not on her donkey, stood looking over its neck into the camera. Her expression was amused and suspicious at once, as if she knew that she, as much as the donkey, was part of the show. A toddler so small that I couldn't believe that it would have been able to support its own weight was physically strapped into the saddle.

The outfits of the donkey-men were curious. A proud-looking man wore a suit, the photo too desaturated to show if sand had filled the cuffs. His slicked hair gleamed in the sun. Two in flat caps. Another with socks pulled up over his trousers, all the way to the knee. The photographs had been gathered from across time, though there were no dates, only changing outfits, ending in T-shirts. I chose a few, leaning towards the strangest.

The rest of the day was the usual tourist admin, hoovering, taking out the bins. A child threw up onto the Perspex display case of Roman plates.

As I was preparing to head out, I saw them through the window – Charlie and M. That was the thing about our town, you were always seeing people you knew. It wasn't remarkable or even coincidental. It was the way things were. You'd see a classmate buying toothpaste or tampons or a pregnancy test and you'd nod to each other. Charlie and M were just walking. He was her best friend, and they were walking together. So what? But she was laughing. She was laughing the way Leo did, her face all surprise and delight. Why was M not at home with F and Leo or in her consultation room, but walking down the street with Charlie? I watched them until they strolled out of view going who knows where.

The Allotments

After work, I headed to the chippie where Mark from my year was helping his mum who was the manager there. He gave me an extra shovel of chips and three packs of vinegar – my usual order. The chips came in a squeaky polystyrene box. I carried them down to the sea wall. The tourists were packing up soggy children. A dog ran along, pebbles leaping up behind its toes. I didn't see M or Charlie again, but I texted F to say I was out with friends. I had no curfew – that endless trope of American TV. F and M expected me to text that I was alive. *We're not building walls for you to kick down,* is what M said. And *Freedom,* was F's word.

It was a while before I saw anyone I knew. But then two girls from my French division walked down the pier, bottles clinking in a plastic bag. We weren't friends but we knew each other well enough that they stopped. They told me that they'd heard our French teacher was getting a divorce and we sat and watched the waves. I sipped at the foamy top of the beer they gave me. Then we were talking about what our French teacher would be like in bed, wrinkling our noses and making orgasm noises with a guttural *r*. On her second beer, one of the girls, Ellie, showed us the face her ex used to make, crossing her eyes and opening her mouth in the O of someone smoking a cigar.

Were you glad you did it? You know, with him?

About half our year had lost their virginity. I wasn't taking any social risks by letting her know where I stood.

I don't know why people make such a fuss. Ellie tossed her hair and the wind took the motion, rippling it outwards. *The first time's not great but it's not too bad either. It's not worse than waxing.*

Around nine, I told them I had to go. I still had most of my chips and decided to keep them in case Andrew wanted cold vinegary potato.

The allotment gate was padlocked. I lodged the polystyrene box under my armpit to climb over. The allotments were tidy. Each square was accompanied by a wooden shed greyed with age or painted broccoli green. The vegetable tents of translucent plastic billowed in the breeze. The only sign of disorder was the burnt sheds. Three of them near the back, seared down to carcasses. Weeds pushed up through the floors. Arson, or so the local paper had said. *Youths.* I was a little embarrassed to not know which ones. It was said that all the towns of the district were pockmarked by such fires. Always by youths, as if being young was enough to explain the burning. A more satisfying explanation I supposed than some grandad's cigarette.

I ate more chips while I waited for Andrew to come up the hill. I checked the time on F's watch. I didn't know why I'd taken it anymore. And I wondered if I should bury it here with the tomatoes. I imagined time sprouting up above it.

Andrew walked towards me with a pendulum swing to his spine. In the summer months, the sun softened the night for hours. It was easy to make out his shape.

When he reached me, he held out a packet of Monster Munch.

No thanks, already well supplied with carbs. I gestured to the chips.

Suit yourself. He put a paw-shaped crisp on his tongue and crushed it between his teeth.

We lay back on the grass which was damp, but I didn't mind.

What's the longest you've ever stayed awake? I asked. *Or . . . the least you've ever slept?*

Three hours, maybe two.

The longest anyone ever stayed awake was eleven days, I told him. *Eleven days.*

I pulled out my phone and showed him the picture of Randy Gardner. The photo was black and white. He had a thick jaw and strong shoulders that showed through his shirt. The article said he was only seventeen. He looked older. It was the 60s, but his hair was thick at the top and short at the sides – Randy was no hippy. I sometimes think of Randy and wonder if sleep came easy to him the rest of his life. Or if those eleven nights flicked a switch in him.

There might be other people who stayed up longer. But the Guinness World Records won't record them because they're worried about the health consequences, I said.

I told him the news about the French teacher's divorce. I plucked a ribbon of grass and wound it around my finger. The air smelt cool and damp and of soil. The smells of the shed-fires had long gone.

Do you want to have sex? I asked. *I mean you don't have to. If you're not into it or something that's fine. Or, I don't know, if you like someone else?* It was not the slick-est seduction.

You don't think it would be strange?

It's fine. It was a stupid idea.

No – And he put his hand on mine. It was warm, even if I could feel the texture of Monster Munch grease.

I looked down at his jeans because girls were always joking about seeing someone's stiffy and oddly I never could. I always assumed it was some fold in the fabric. I wasn't sure that I saw anything different.

I don't think you want me to describe the fumbling or the teeth clicking. Or maybe I don't want to. Because it wasn't bad sex, not the way people mean it in comedy routines. The grass and pebbles rubbed against my back. Above us the sky darkened. My phone hummed with texts, but I didn't reach out to check it. It was painful but not miserable and I liked how close his face was to mine. I wondered for a moment if I had made a mistake. If I should have acted coyer. I wondered if I was doing this for the wrong reasons. He smelt like a teenage boy but also warmer and fresher, like the difference between mud and mud after a light rain. He kept asking, *Is this okay?* His hands – so steady with a pencil – were hesitant, as if afraid that they might make a mark that would ruin the whole composition. At one point he touched my ear and it felt like he was holding all of me and another time I had to ask him to move because there was a rock in my back.

Later whenever I saw a candle blown out, the wick a short black stub, I would think of the burnt sheds. I would imagine two tiny people lying in the white belly of the candle wax side by side figuring out what to do. Though I usually avoid remembering how I took his hand and slid it towards my neck and held it there. I waited for him to press or for a jag of pain. Even as I felt Andrew inside me I was looking for a scale, a ruler with which to measure the things I'd seen. But Andrew pulled the hand away and pushed it into my hair and I was too nervous to ask him to put it back.

It was done and I wasn't a virgin anymore, which felt not so different from being a virgin. I looked over at Andrew to see if something had changed between us.

Was it nice? I asked.

Yes, he said.

I wondered why he hadn't made a move on me before? Weren't boys supposed to always be trying to push their way inside?

Oh, he said. And scrambled towards his satchel. He pulled out a sketchbook. The cover was barely marked and the ribbon that stuck its tongue from between the sheets was unfrayed. He opened it to a page that was almost entirely black with ink. But he'd left gaps of white that looked like stars. In the centre, a girl flew, her hair billowing out around her. She wore pyjamas. She looked into an open window, though it was too dark to see any of the house, only the window's white grid.

I drew your dream.

Oh. It made me oddly wistful. *I didn't fly. I just walked.*

Maybe you should try flying next time. He squeezed my hand.

Don't draw tonight's adventure, okay?

I lay beside him in the grass. It was hard to read his expression in the dark. But I felt him pull me in closer. We talked for a long time about nothing much. Hours. Mostly it was Andrew asking me about the plot of his kraken comic, if I thought it made sense, was too simple or too complicated. I traced the plot arc along his arm. I don't know which one of us fell asleep first. But we woke up to the sound of gulls and with the hush of rain on our faces. My phone was dead and I lifted F's watch close to my eyes trying to make out the time.

It's three. Andrew's phone was still alive and lighting up his face, ghostly sour.

I hadn't dreamt but I hadn't left my body either. I wondered if Andrew had anchored me. He offered to walk me home but I said it would be better not to. When it was time to split we both paused for a moment. The choices hung between us. To kiss? To hug? To walk off? Then Andrew raised a hand in a jaunty salute. I bowed and turned towards home.

Two Fleas

F was waiting at the end of the front path. It was too dark to see his expression. The tall shape of my father ran its hands along the top of its scalp.

He started to talk before I could even get close.

You didn't answer your phone.

I didn't feel like it.

It was late. It was almost satisfying to see his anger. Clear against the night, beaming straight at me. It was almost good to be in the full heat of it, not hovering in the dark peripheries.

You were gone all night.

It's still night. I kept my voice steady and insolent, ready to take more and more of it.

Where were you?

With Andrew.

He stopped for a moment as if he had been expecting some other answer. Something more or less palatable. Then he started again, telling me that I'd upset my mother and Leo. That Leo hadn't been able to sleep and kept asking where I'd gone.

Leo? Really? Leo's opinion counts? You're as bad as M.

Fine. I couldn't sleep.

You never sleep. Can we go inside now? I'm cold.

F held the gate open. *Is Andrew your boyfriend?*

He's my friend.

Really, your friend?

You can have male friends.

You can . . . His voice was disbelieving.

M does. Isn't Charlie like her best-best-best friend? Isn't that why we moved here?

We moved here because there's a good school and fresh air. F's voice was measured and calm.

Which Charlie told you about.

Stop changing the topic.

What if I don't want to?

Were you doing things with this Andrew?

Do you mean was I drunk? Or high? A doubt squirmed. I didn't want to have this conversation, didn't want F to imagine me this way.

Were you?

Why does it matter?

You're a child.

Was I having sex? Did I have his dick in my mouth, is that what you're asking? Or was it inside of me? I couldn't make the words stop. They flew wildly from my mouth. I'd never spoken to anyone like this. *What's the big deal?*

You're my child.

It's not as if it is sacred. You don't believe in that stuff? Remember? Your God doesn't have rules . . .

F closed his eyes. He let out a long breath.

Sometimes, I feel God. Not like a man. A huge animal thing. I feel it breathing. It's like being a flea on an animal that only notices you when it scratches.

139

Then he reached out and held me. So close. So tight to his chest that my nose bent on its side.

Caterpillar, I thought you were hurt.

I reached into my pocket and handed him back his watch.

4

In order to tell the truth, I am lying to you, telling you I have to work late. I am writing this instead of sitting at your kitchen table eating pasta with onions simmered to brown-sweetness. I know I will not be able to watch you read. But with each sentence I write, I imagine the face you will make. Sometimes, I can't do it. I simply don't know how you'll rearrange your features.

I told myself that I didn't talk about that town because of the sleep watching, because it would make me seem deluded. I thought that was why I never spoke about F and what happened between us, because to speak about F, I'd have to tell you about my mind leaving my body. But it might be the other way around.

143

Doubles

I found myself outside my body. Daylight falling over the bedroom. This was the first time my body and I had split in the day. But my body seemed to want to catch up on the rest it had missed during my night with Andrew. Leo was lying in the middle of our bedroom floor rearranging his Lego men. He was playing a game he called *Theatre*. The stage was built using red bricks. But other than that, it was like any child's game: heroes and villains. The only difference was that even the Lego men knew they were pretending.

Looking at him lying on his stomach, I wondered if I was failing him. He was muttering to the Lego men. Sound came from him in a wiggling, whispery sing-song. He was trying, I thought, to let the body in the bed rest. The eldest were supposed to take care of the youngest and I pitied him then. In so many of his books, siblings went off on adventures together to fight the demons. In a way, I had gone to Never Never Land without him. Except, I hadn't gone anywhere. This was our house. I could hear someone moving about downstairs.

In clear day I expected my out-of-body self to look different, as if the sun would display my unreality. But going down the stairs, I was only myself. F had painted the banister a few years ago but since then Leo had left his fingerprints on the spindles. Tiny smudges from where he'd pulled himself up or down. The rail felt hard and smooth. I lifted my hand and flung it through, as hard and fast as I could go.

It went.

I never saw my hand inside the banister. It was like those Victorian toys – zoetropes which, when spun, show a jerky animation. The human eye is fast enough to see something is not quite right, but not enough to decide what is wrong. The night before hovered at the edge of my mind: F's face of confusion as he took his watch and slid it back into his pocket. He had peered at me with worry but had not asked why.

I was hungry but I didn't think this self could eat cereal. I didn't know you could be hungry without a stomach. I remembered the sound and went down to see what was going on. It was coming from F's study. This confused me because he usually only woke up in time for lunch. Then as I slipped in through the open door, I saw M opening and closing drawers. She leafed through files and records. She had a small stack of papers on the floor beside her. On the top was a letter from our school, though it was dated a year before. I remembered that letter, it was about the way Leo was always late for school. F had laughed about it, but M had called them in an apologetic voice. And after that I'd had to take Leo to his school on the way to mine. The summer had been a reprieve from this commute. I feel guilty for resenting those few extra streets now. I leant over the paper, rereading the scolding school language. *Cause for concern* etc., etc.

When I looked up, she had our passports, all four. Leo didn't have one yet. He'd never been anywhere. But when

I was a baby, they'd driven me across the Channel and down the coast to Portugal. They'd applied for both my passports at once, American and British, to get it out of the way. I don't remember it, but sometimes Portugal appeared in F's songs. Usually, the word rose at the end as if climbing closer to the sky.

M flipped open the fronts of the passports. The first was her own. People are supposed to look ugly in passport photos. She looked fine. A little bleached maybe. Her mouth unsmiling, as regulations dictated. She looked proud, dignified even, like the Queen on the stamps. M put the passport on top of the rest of her things. F's passport was next. She saw his thumb-sized face and flipped it right back down. Then there were two left. By default, both me. She held one in each hand. The books were identical in size and similar in gilding. She put one on my father's passport and one on hers. Splitting me as easily as a lump of dough. She put F and American me back in the drawer where she had found the passports. And the other pile, her pile, she stowed onto the very top of the tallest cabinet.

She stopped, looking up at it. She wound her wedding ring around her finger, left and then right. She opened the drawer again and placed both of me with her.

Then she walked upstairs and woke me up. Yanked back into myself, I blinked up at her but her expression gave nothing away.

Swim

M walked into the museum with our duffel bag swung over her shoulder.

You're done soon? she asked.

In ten, I told her. I pretended to be busy. I wasn't, or not with anything that mattered. The museum had a lot of leaflets for places up and down the coast but the leaflets had different attitudes towards time. Some, usually the ones in tasteful colours with pictures of great houses and daffodils, aspired towards eternity. They spoke of long truths, the house's age, its gardens, things that had happened in 1709. The other type used a great many exclamation marks and wished to tell you about not-to-be-missed events! Both leaflets had a day of death. The former, when the text began to go grey and the paper wrinkled. The latter, when the events mentioned had ended – bouncy castles deflated, tours disbanded, cake macerated to crumbs. I was dispatching these. Cassandra had warned me not to be too harsh. If some weren't kept on life support our display might look too meagre. I stared at these leaflets instead of looking at M, who I did not want to be there, watching me as if I were Leo's age.

Cassandra came out of the office. Her face twitched with a recognition that M often received. I'd seen it enough times to know the questions that usually followed. *Are you . . .?* or *You're . . .?* Each leaving space for M to volunteer the origin of her skin and face and eyes. The lineage that was not quite English or at least, not Pict, not Roman, not Viking, not Norman. Something other. Cassandra had never looked at me with so much interest. My face took after F's.

Cassandra asked her version of the question, weaving in her own story of how she'd come here for university and never left. M unspooled the Kyushu story again – English father, Japanese mother etc . . . Then Cassandra said, *It's funny. I guess you're a bit like your dad then?*

What? M placed the duffel on the floor between her feet.

You said your dad went to Japan and took himself home a wife? And Kit tells me her dad is American. So you went and got yourself a husband?

M reached up and touched the neat bun at the back of her head as if looking for reassurance that it was still there.

I suppose I never thought of it like that. M glanced at me. *I wasn't looking for a husband, just a road trip and some good photographs.*

You went alone? Cassandra asked.

I've always liked travelling alone. I used to hike all over the country when I was young. Though that was the last real trip . . .

Well, thanks, I said. *I apologise for interrupting your travel plans.* It unsettled me to hear them chatting. Cassandra was closer to my age than M's but they were easier together than I knew how to be.

The clock was already quite far past five by the time we left.

We're going swimming, M said.

Don't have my swimming costume.

In the bag.

The quiet beach was a half hour walk away. In English, *to walk to* is to travel with a goal at the end and *to take a walk* is to move for its own sake. It would have been easy for M to pick me up in the car and we could have arrived in five minutes. Taking a walk meant she wanted to talk.

It wasn't long before she said, *So you're seeing a boy?*

M loved a vague question. She did this when I got a school report saying I hadn't tried hard in Maths too. *I want to let you speak for yourself,* was how she'd put it. But if she wanted me to talk to her about Andrew, she was going to have to work for it.

What makes you think that?

Well, from what your dad said it didn't sound like a girl. But we're fine with that too.

Mmm . . .

You know as well as anyone that for me the main factor was never gender or genitalia or even long hair versus short. It was Andrew's gentleness that I wanted. I thought of the way he looped his fingers through mine as we walked home in the dark.

What else did my parents say to each other, do to each other, when I wasn't watching? It felt as though no matter how hard I kept watch on them, they were always finding ways to slip around behind my back.

You're using protection?

Yes.

What sort?

I don't want to talk about it.

She looked at me long and steady, and I could feel myself shrinking and curling and twisting back into her womb and splitting into two pieces and being dropped into the drain – unmade.

Is he kind to you? It's Andrew, right?

What?

Is he kind? she repeated.

The things he wanted to do were quiet and hurt no one. He never laughed at the crueller jokes people made, but I wasn't sure if that was from discretion or because he was thinking about krakens instead.

Of course, he is. You know him.

You can't always tell from the outside. But that's good. It's good if the first one is kind. People can fall into bad patterns. I see it all the time. They get treated badly young and then they think that's how they should get treated.

No one is treating me badly.

We walked in silence until we'd passed the baker, the shelves now empty of iced buns and lemon drizzle and cinnamon rolls.

Was your first one kind? I asked.

M stopped as if considering, then she said, *Yes, he was very kind. He bought me sunflowers afterwards. I hung them upside down in my room to dry.*

Was it Charlie? The image of his tall body curled over hers flashed into my head.

No, why would you ask that? No, this was when I was still in secondary school. Your age, actually.

I was hungry and she told me she had almonds in a Ziploc in the duffle. I was not an almond person. Their skin is papery and the inside like candle wax. I ate five.

M said we should really swim while the water was warm. Though it was never all that warm. She stripped to her black one piece and then held the towel up. We'd done this since I was a child, M making a tent with only a beach towel and her body, to hide me from the world. I ducked under her arms into the nubby cotton cave. I was close enough that I could see the green veins under her skin, the small sunspots, and the bruises on her shoulder which had darkened and mottled to the purple-brown of cooked chicken thigh. The bruises whose cause I thought I knew.

Had it been that bad? Or were these from something else, some other moment that I'd missed? I was always bruising from knocking too fast into lockers or turning clumsily against the side of the pool. I once had a blue spot where Leo accidentally sprinted over my foot. How hard did something have to be to bruise?

It was my first time seeing them in daylight. It should have felt like a confirmation, but what was the joy in that? Triumph that I wasn't delusional? I tugged off my jeans and underwear first, pulling my costume up to my belly.

Your shoulder, I said, as I pulled my shirt off. In the huddle of the towel, not looking into her face but over her shoulder, it felt possible to say this.

It's nothing, she said. She paused, her face almost completely still. Perhaps the muscles under the purple dots moved slightly. I wasn't sure. *Swimming,* she added. *There was a lot of grit in the water.*

But I think she knew that I knew because she looked almost ashamed. She whipped the towel away as soon as I was changed. We lodged our duffel between two rocks. We'd done this enough times in this spot and it had never

151

been stolen. Then she was jogging down to the sea, loose strands from her bun flapping in her wake, and I was chasing her into the waves.

A shiver flew over my skin as I hit the water. Swimming in the sea and swimming in a pool are quite different. In the pool, the lane markers are always there to tell you how you are doing and with each slam against the end comes a sense of a pace being set and progress being made. Of course, it is easier in a pool to tell when you are losing. The others sit on the plastic benches watching, their hair tucked up into caps, like a row of judgemental monks.

When they say the sea is fathomless, they mean it is deep. But to me it was not its size which intimidated but its lack of clear pathways. You could swim and swim and not notice as the tide had whisked you East or West. You could get nowhere or you could be carried out and away.

M kicked forwards and I raced after the blue-green pads of her feet.

M had taught me to swim, had held me in flotation wings. She had promised not to let go. And then at some point she had. My nose and eyes had filled with salt, I could taste it right up in my eyeballs. But she'd made sure I could swim and afterwards she'd told me, *Now you can never drown.* It had become our thing, not drowning together. Sometimes it seemed like the only thing we had after Leo was born.

As we were walking back up the hill, towels around our necks, she asked me, *If you had to leave this place, would you be sad?*

I'm going to uni in two years.

152

I meant before that. I know this is where your friends are.

Why?

Your father . . . she paused. *Other than the band, there's not much for him here. I thought perhaps a change . . .*

I could move, I said.

Cosmomagical

I wished we were back at school with its peeling linoleum floors and grey carpets designed to show no stains. It would be easier to run into Andrew accidentally, casually. There was a girl I had thought of being at the beginning of the year, a girl who gifted her body in a careful and measured way. This was the closest I had ever been to hating him. Not because he hadn't texted me. He had, the day after, a photograph of a doodle of himself inside a small cartoon cage and his mother swinging a key. His mother's face was a mask of anger, wiggles of steam coming out from the ears. I hadn't replied and this was why I hated him. Because without warning I remembered a movie, or was it a TV show, or was it something that I had overheard, that you weren't supposed to text for two days. And now because we'd pressed our bodies together, I found myself caring about such rules and so I hated him and didn't text and instead watched M and F like they were two otters I'd tagged for biological study, but with no co-scientist.

Sleep watching, staring at my parents, should have used up all of my emotion. And yet I checked my phone at all times of day. Cassandra rolled her eyes and told me to clean the museum toilet. I thought of Andrew as the blue liquid poured down the yellow porcelain. I thought of M as I scraped the white plastic bristles up and down the bowl. I thought of F as I leant against the graffitied wall and closed my eyes and tried to remember what he looked like happy. I decided that if Andrew texted me again, I could reply. He didn't. I set a timer on my phone for when I could write. It went off and I didn't text.

I walked to his house. I had done it enough times before and I told myself there was no reason to be scared of him now. I patted the bent-trunked apple tree for reassurance and rang his doorbell.

His mother answered the door.

Ms Murty, hi. I wasn't expecting her. She was never in. What I liked best about her house was the lack of adults. I couldn't ask her why she wasn't at the hospital. So I stood on the doorstep while she asked me about my parents and my summer. I was uncertain whether this short woman wearing thick white athletics socks knew I'd had sex with her son.

When enough pleasantries had been extracted, she let me up the stairs. He was drawing, his face close to the page. When he saw me, he looked up and smiled and everything in his face was easy and welcoming. I wondered if I should kiss it. I wondered if those were the sorts of people we were now.

He put his pen down when he saw me.

Hi.

Hi.

I sat on the floor by his feet. Pencil shavings arrow-headed the carpet. I played with one while I told him that we might be moving. That I didn't know when. He slid down next to me.

Where are you going?

I shrugged again and then said, *Away?*

If it's LA, then I'm coming with you.

I don't think we're going to LA.

You should.

What would I do in LA?

Help me write my movie.

I can't write a movie.

You wouldn't have to do the hard parts, just the dialogue.

Isn't it all dialogue?

Well, I believe in you, he said and ran a thumb over the back of my hand.

His plan for our collaboration had predated fucking or even the idea of fucking. It emerged when we were the only two children Ms Fairchild let use the good brushes, because we were slow and patient. I used to write the captions on his pictures. Most of the captions were either *Ahhhhhhhh* or *Arrrghhhhhhhh*. The sounds of the killed and the killer. I suppose it was his way of making it so that it wouldn't be a competition between us: for the best brushes, the best paints, the only tube of truly opaque white. We'd collaborate and not compete. At first, he said it should be a graphic novel, but lately he'd decided it should be a movie.

He leant against me and I let this image hang between us. Our future in LA painted in gold and cobalt. My head on his shoulder, as it was now but under a sunnier sky. My loyal, sweet boyfriend. People would try to get between us but fail because we shared this original town.

Okay, I said. *But only if, when you sell our movie, we can get a pool.*

I learnt a new word today, he said. *Cosmomagical. Cosmo magical.*

What?

The magic of the cosmos. It's the magic you make with the stars and the city. Like when Ancient Chinese planners laid out their towns to please the heavens. You have to find a moment to put that in our movie.

I told him that I was pretty sure this place was laid out to please the council or the tourists. His unmade movie was about our town. He'd been working on the sketches as long as I'd known him.

Use your imagination. Our movie will have monsters that live under the sea and mermaids that pull tourists to their deaths and phoenixes that set fire to garden sheds. And girls who fly.

If you love it so much, why go to America?

If you tried telling people here about this place, no one would be interested. That's why we have to tell strangers. We'll tell them about our town by the sea and all its monsters.

I told you, I wasn't flying. It felt strange to think of this place as my hometown and not just my town.

He tugged up the back of my shirt. Only the back was lifted, the front caught around the bottom of my bra. I swatted at his hands, less because I minded and more because I felt like he shouldn't do it so easily.

Turn that way, he said. I felt the soft touch of a marker against the skin of my upper back. It tickled and I squirmed but he used the other hand to keep my shoulder steady. The tip moved in curves. Fast. The ink was a little cold. Then it stopped and he reached up for his phone.

No, I said, *use mine.* I had been drilled in protecting your image. A security precaution that was futile as I'd told Andrew my phone's code years ago. He asked me to hold my shirt up and I did, crossing my arms over my chest to do it. When he handed me the photo, I saw that he'd drawn on my back a small pair of scaled wings.

Scales?

Would you rather have feathers? he asked. I shook my head and kissed him.

For the Record

The wings took two weeks to fade. I showered but he'd used indelible ink. Life continued as they disappeared.

Here are some things I saw when I night-walked –

Leo sleeping, a line of drool running over the curve of his cheek and making a mouse-size puddle on the sheet.

A neighbour hunting slugs by the beam of her torch. Boot coming down hard on their wet bodies.

A rat going into a bin in the town's centre, his tail curving over the edge.

M sleeping on her side, curling up like a terrier, paws curled under.

F sleeping, lying on his back with his mouth open.

Andrew painting. His fingers gathering new blots of ink.

F grabbing M by the arm as she left a room.

Arguments about F's work. M asking why it wasn't happening.

Once, F putting his hand over M's mouth and holding it there. Begging her, *Be quiet. Please. Please just stop.*

M crying, only once, very quietly.

M bent over her computer while F talked to her.

F singing loudly alone in the kitchen.

F kissing M, holding her tight and close.

M pulling away.

Sometimes I wondered if there was a golden amount of whisky that might allow F to see the half-ghost of his daughter sitting on the kitchen counter-top watching him. I tried to remember if there were hints from before I'd night-walked. When had F's hands started holding on so tight? I had no idea. During the day, things seemed as they had been the year before and the year before that. The beach looked fuller and fuller each day. I met up with girls from school who reported on the tourists their parents were hosting in spare rooms. There were men who hung around outside my friends' bedroom doors and couples who copulated loudly, their cries pouring through the walls.

At work, Cassandra asked me about the Sun Songs. Halfway through my explanation, she started smearing coconut lip balm over her bottom lip. The strong perfumy smell tangled with the stink of old carpets and I felt a little woozy. I finished up the explanation quickly, *So yeah. My dad joined a local band when we first moved here. He's not exactly the leader but he writes all the songs. The real leader, Peter, he's covered in smurf tattoos and stupid things. And he always wants to do covers. Says the crowd prefers them. They used to play together more but I guess my dad and Peter have been fighting. But the band do Sun Songs every year.*

She told me that F should come in. We could record his songs for the archive. I asked what she meant and she asked if I'd been to the Science Museum in London. I hadn't. And she said that in contemporary curating it was

160

believed that it was more powerful to have different sorts of exhibit, to engage the other senses. She had ordered a second-hand tablet and she reckoned we could keep it by the front desk and people could listen to interesting things on it – the sounds of seabirds, wartime radio broadcasts, my father singing.

I said, *Oh.*

I thought about F being unhappy here. Perhaps the problem was that he spent too much time singing alone in the dark. I told her that I'd ask.

I think I'm going to adopt two kittens, she said. *My neighbour had kittens, well her cat did.*

Cool.

I want to call them Sturm and Drang. But my girlfriend thinks that's pretentious and wants to call them Gilbert and George. What's your vote?

I think if my boyfriend adopted a cat, he'd call it Cthulhu, I said and I rolled the taste of *boyfriend* around my mouth.

I had sex with Andrew again and again in his house. It was fun learning the fit of our bodies. His genitals smelt faintly floral, which I had not expected. Though it made more sense when I found his mother's rose-scented moisturiser in the bathroom. I dabbed it on my wrist and whirled it around. After we were done, I lay on his chest which was smooth and hairless. Once, I pressed my face into the seam in his rib cage and when he asked what I was doing I told him I was trying to smell his spirit.

Another time, when I was on top of him, I put my hands around his neck.

161

Is this okay? I asked.

He made a small and ragged noise. He nodded.

The skin there was the smoothest anywhere on his body. I was careful to avoid the soft centre. I pressed my thumbs into the sides. He held my hips. I could feel him moving, alive underneath me. I could not feel what pain he might have felt. Obvious, perhaps, but it surprised me how difficult it was to tell what effect those thumbs were having. I pressed harder, shifting my weight forwards. I watched his face looking for signs. His mouth was slightly open, the breath heavy. I could feel it moving up his throat. It was strange to hold the source of his life under me. His eyes were slightly wider open than normal, silvery and wet.

Afterwards, he asked, *What was that about?*

Did you like it?

I don't know, he said.

Were you scared?

Do you want me to be?

It was difficult to imagine anyone being scared of me. I shook my head. He caught one of the strands of my hair and wrapped it around his fingers.

If I leave, even if it's not LA, will you visit me? I asked.

Of course, he said, and I felt an ache that he'd agreed so easily.

You don't know where I'm going. It could be some island in the north of Scotland.

I wanted to tell him everything. After all, he was the one who told me that in all the old magic stories, naming a thing gives you power over it.

I wrapped my hand around his, less from affection and more because I wanted a warning if he was going to move.

Our palms were tepid as the food they served at school. For the first time, he seemed weak – only a boy, with long eyelashes and faint acne scars. Not someone I could ask to hold everything that I had seen.

In my doubt, I saw him as I imagined I might from the secure future of adulthood – a silly boy obsessed with monsters because his mother was never home. Though this is not how I see him now at all. Now, it is hard to remember him as anything but beautiful and bursting with creatures.

I didn't think I could explain about F. How could I say that my father might be the sort of man you were supposed to get help from and also say that he seemed so sad? Maybe, eventually, I'd have the right words for what was happening between M and F. But at least I could tell Andrew about the way I had been splitting. I laid it out carefully, not in as much detail as I have given you of course. I told him of the watching and of the gathering of evidence. I took pains to tell him of experiments that had been done on those who had out-of-body experiences. How they had given them electric shocks. People had been flung out of their bodies and onto ceilings. How scientists believed that this meant out-of-body experiences were electricity misfiring. But couldn't it be possible that they were demonstrating the opposite? The mind's ability to escape?

His room smelt of orange peel. I wondered if there was any fruit left. I wished I could sneak into his mind and F's and M's. I wanted to see, not their rooms, but their cerebrums. I wanted to watch their electrical signals jump. I wanted to know if he believed me.

I pressed myself closer to him, as if in this way, I could seep into him. He listened. He asked questions. The questions did not hint at suspicion. They were about what I had eaten beforehand (which I knew) and what phase of the moon it had been (which I didn't).

Do you feel like a witch?

Not really?

A monster?

Maybe.

He said, *I always knew you were special.*

I was happy feeling his body crescent around mine. Really happy – the sort of happiness where you are afraid to move and lose it. Andrew hadn't doubted me. I pressed my head against his chest. His breath buoyed me up and down ever so slightly.

I asked why he had never made a move on me, which wasn't strictly relevant, but which felt important to know and we were being honest. He looked at the ceiling and bit his lip and said, *I guess I didn't want to be a dick.* Fair enough. He said that he always used cheap sketchbooks. For Christmas every year, his mother gave him a good one with thick paper but he'd spend all year avoiding it. It was too nice and he would feel afraid of wasting this good paper. When he did draw in them, the drawings were stiff and awkward. His hand didn't flow. I smiled. It was the first time in our friendship that he had told me about being scared. He said in a lower, quieter voice that he'd been thinking and maybe this was why he hadn't. He stopped but I knew what he meant. I wondered if we would be stiff together. I became stiff. Stiff even in my toes.

Kit?

Yes.

I'm glad that we're together, you know.

Together, I said and let myself soften against him. Together. It sounds like to gather, doesn't it? And that's how I felt then. Gathered up.

Song

F and I sat in his study, him on the chair and me on the short filing cabinet. The cold edge dug into my thigh. My phone balanced on a pile of books in front of F. We were recording a test sample to play for Cassandra. I didn't know if Cassandra was thinking of studio quality or if some staticky mumbly thing would strike her as more authentic. I tried to explain this to F. It was strange to think that Cassandra would decide whether or not F's song was good enough. I wondered what would happen if it wasn't. I felt cold, despite the sun coming through the window. The dust – there was a lot of dust in that room – hung in the air.

F was fiddling with his guitar, and tapping his foot. He played a few chords. He nodded to me that he was ready to start. I pressed the red circle to begin. The notes rose clear and bright. The sounds were the ones that I had been hearing for weeks. I hadn't caught the words yet. I hoped he would choose the bright playful lyrics that his band preferred and not one of his lonely God songs. He took longer than usual to open his mouth. And then the words arrived. They were about M. You might not have known if you heard. You might have thought it was a generic love song. But I was sure. He sung with his eyes closed. Was he imagining M's face? Or the crowd on the beach? Or neither? I wondered if M could hear – it was a Sunday and she was home.

If you like, I'll sing you this song. I remember it. It sounded the way sun catching the top of a wall looks, or the way someone holding your hand on a cold day feels. But if I try to write it out here, I am worried it will seem a thin little thing with so few words. You need the music, you see.

Listening to it, I was proud of him. Can you understand that? In all those nights I'd been watching, I had somehow missed this? This beauty. And it made me feel like maybe I had missed other things. Other secret kindnesses.

Which was about the time that Leo came into the room. Leo who was singing his own song high and loud, only it wasn't his own song, it was the song of a cartoon show. Leo who had rings of gold around his eyes, and who would someday be in an advertisement for praline ice cream. Leo. The miracle child.

F stopped singing.

Leo warbled like he was the sunny centre of the world. F put down the guitar and leant it against the wall. Leo stopped singing. And I was aware again of the metal cabinet on my legs. The chill of it. I don't know where M had been, but quickly she was behind Leo. As if summoned by the quiet.

What's going on? she said in her calm therapist's voice.

Your son interrupted. F was still holding the guitar pick, the skin under his thumb gone white from squeezing. And then he chucked the pick, not exactly at Leo but near him. It bounced off the wall and slid to the ground. His arm hung loose.

Leo stepped back and towards M. I felt my bones try to move closer to my spine. F stood and brushed past me, his body knocking against mine as if it was not there. He stopped close to M. His eyes were fixed on the space between Leo and M, a small patch of white wall.

My palms pressed against the cool metal of the filing cabinet. *We can start again,* I said. *It's fine.*

F didn't look at me.

He's got to learn to respect other people's space, F said. He metered out the words one after the other with a metronome's insistence.

I noticed the pink gutters under M's eyes – wet and swollen somehow. Her voice raised. *You could've blinded him.*

He told her to *fuck off.* He asked her, *How can you say that? I could never. I would never hurt my family.*

Leo's face turned red and streaky as a gala apple. A few years before he would have cried, but he was learning to keep it in. I wanted to tell him to learn faster.

F was standing very close to M then. His own face was green and white, the larger apple. On the chair, my phone kept recording. The white line jumping as they spoke, like the heartbeat of a very ill person. I waited for him to touch her. He did.

His hand on the place where her neck met her shoulder, her back against the door frame. Asking her again how she could say something like this about him. *Why would you frighten the kids like that?* His hand again on that strip of her throat. Gentle though, resting, like it had fallen there. My own breath paused as if it too was being held.

Then M jerked away, looking over her shoulder to Leo. F caught her wrist, and for a second she seemed like a dancer at the furthest edge of a spin. And then the strain showed on her face. F was still gripping, staring at her.

Don't, I said. They both looked at me, as if they had only just realised I was there. M's expression wobbled before flattening into calm. F let go, shoving his hand into his pocket, and walked out of the room. I heard the front door swing shut behind him.

M bent down to Leo and hugged him. The hug was loose, her arms at obtuse angles. Leo didn't try to escape, only leaning closer. I picked up my phone and ended the recording.

M looked at me and said, *Can you check on your father?* And I wondered how much taller than her I was doomed to be, how much more I would outstrip her. I went to him. He was standing by our front gate, looking out towards the sea, though the sea view was blocked by houses.

My love, I want to tell you how he was feeling. I want to tell you the song in my father's heart as he picked up pebbles one by one and laid them in a line on top of the garden wall. It would be comforting to be able to explain why he'd behaved as he had. To show you the clear lines in which his childhood led to mine. A tidier story. But I don't know and I never will. I've watched videos of men who'd hurt their wives. Men who'd thrown televisions and chairs. Men who'd pulled arms out of sockets. Men who snapped back fingers. These men spoke of fire, of the colour red, of being eaten by rage. I don't know what F would say in one of those groups. I never looked for a group for daughters. I was afraid, I suppose, that their stories would make more sense. That they would have the heroes and villains lined up more tidily. There are so very many men who do worse. Men who are deliberate and considered bullies. Men who kick and stomp and crush their wives, sons, daughters. It is hard for me to talk about this man who was not all bad, or at least I don't think he was. But this is the only story I have.

F, well, he made a river of white pebbles. Then he flicked them off, one by one.

I'm sorry, he said. Plink. Plink. Plink.

I wanted him to say more. I scripted it in my head, moving his face like a puppet. I wanted to tell him that he was my drowning game choice. I wanted to pull him out of the water, but that he needed to give me something.

I said, *Sometimes I get angry. Like everything's fine and then it's not. And I have to do something to make it stop.* I waited for a yes, a recognition.

Is that why you took my watch? he asked.

Maybe. I wasn't really talking about myself. I was providing his lines. But now I think that it is also how I am. Not exactly. Not in the details. But in the rush of adrenaline that tells me to do something, anything, when a certain feeling comes down upon me.

He touched the top of my head and said, *I forgive you, Caterpillar.*

Moving On

That night I watched them both. They moved quietly around each other, never getting too close, as if the broad back of an invisible lion stalked between them. F stacked the dishes, with such gentleness they barely clinked. M worked on her laptop, her fingers moving smoothly as she described other people's sorrows. F boiled the kettle and looked down at her but she only shook her head. Her expression was smooth as a sand dune. She went to bed. F followed not long after. She slept and he lay with the reading lamp on, not reading but looking at the curve of her neck. His expression was one I'd seen friends' dogs make when their humans were eating, a resigned sort of hunger.

I lay my spirit body down at the foot of their bed and closed my eyes. I was awake but not. My mind was ready as a seismograph but I registered only the shifting of feet. I thought back to before Leo was born. The way it had felt to have a room to myself, a space of my own, the way sometimes very early in the morning, I'd wake up before either of them. I could still remember the quiet as I snuck into their room and curled up at the end of the bed like a cat. The air felt different then.

Night passed lethargically. Then, as the gulls woke up, M moved quietly. Getting dressed in the dawn light. She gathered her hair and clipped it back. She did not eat breakfast. But she went into his office and slipped her papers from the top of the cabinet. Then she went to the canvas bag in which we put all our dirty clothes. She took it. Big as it was, the heavy bottom of it swinging, she chucked it into her car. The first thing I thought was that our machine was broken. The second was to wonder if she was going to burn our clothes. The way girls burnt notes their ex-boyfriends had sent them. But that didn't seem like a very M thing to do.

I woke up as she started the car.

On my way to work, I listened to the recording one more time. In the morning air, the song still sounded fresh and bright. I had caught the rest: my brother walking in, F, M, every rasped half sentence. I deleted it. There are some things that hearing twice is too much.

Cassandra had brought a portable speaker into work. She was playing some goth revival, ladies who sounded so sad, like someone had nicked their handbags.

There was another woman standing by the desk. For a moment I thought she was the world's earliest tourist but then I realised that she was the woman from Cassandra's photograph. I introduced myself. And the woman smiled. She told me this was Cassandra's dream job. Cassandra looked embarrassed and shook her head so her fringe flopped back and forth. I told her that we hadn't got around to recording F's song. He had had a big client job. Cassandra explained to her girlfriend that my father was a local folk singer. This wasn't quite accurate and I wondered who told her folk. And then I regretted deleting the song. It would have been possible to crop it. To play right up until the moment that everything went wrong. Only I would have known what was coming.

The girlfriend offered me a fruit cup. She had bought far too much for the train. The sweet mingled fruit acids were pleasant. I thanked her.

Cassandra left early to show her girlfriend the town. I sat in the swivel chair, swivelling, wondering who discovered that people would be too lazy to stand and turn. Andrew texted me a picture. It was a girl, her torso coming through a door. Her eyes were two fast dots of a pen. Her mouth was smiling.

He texted, *you can always come over.*

I replied, *Thx.*

Then M walked through the door. Her hair was tumble tangled. There were new bruises on her right wrist. Four red marks. Once M told me that in Japan four was an unlucky number. It was a pun for death.

She told me quietly and without drama that we were leaving. That I was to go back to the house and put my most precious things into a bag without fuss. That she'd taken the laundry. *There will be something to wear at least. But if there is anything you'd miss you should grab that. You don't need to say anything to him. I'll deal with that. Don't forget your laptop charger. Your phone.*

Though she spoke quietly and evenly, something about the words jangled. She could've been telling me to prepare for a holiday in the Peak District. But her expression was so focused, as if each word was a dart that she was using her entire concentration to aim. I found it hard to look at her eyes so I reread the British Seabirds poster. The artist had drawn some flying and some sitting or swimming. I wondered whether it was easier for them to be on the land, in the air or on the water. Were all of those things equally comfortable for them?

You don't have to be like this. Sneaky.

Kit. M closed her eyes for a moment as if counting out a beat. And then she held up her arm. Turning to display each oval. She asked me if I understood.

Yes but . . . I wanted to say that he wasn't dangerous. Danger was the man who hits you over the head with a brick. Danger was the guy who spits in your face and kicks you in the belly. F was different. Whatever he'd done, wasn't he different? I didn't say those things.

Into the silence, M said, *Kit, I'm tired. I thought . . . I thought. I can't anymore okay. I can't and still be me. He's your father but* . . .

Instead I asked, *When did it start?*

I suppose part of me thought that when the chair had fallen, something had broken in him, and in me. That we'd become dislodged together. You once explained to me the concept of the inciting incident. The thing that happens that kicks a story off, the moment everything changes – this is the moment a story begins. Although I didn't have the word for it then, I think that's what I wanted. An inciting incident, a moment that made everything different. That's what I wanted her to tell me. If I knew what moment, I might know how to reverse things.

M said, *I loved the man he was with you.*

So, always? I asked.

Not always.

Cassandra had left the window open to get the carpet smell out of the room. But despite the famously clean sea air, I could also smell the industrial rubbish bin that was parked up right near the museum. It had been cooking in the hot sun all week.

M told me that he had been good with me. That he loved me. But that these moods came upon him. That when she was at work, he seemed to feel choked by her absence. When she came home, he'd hold her until it hurt. She said these things and they all sounded strangely generic, both too dramatic and too benign. The marks on her arm had more colour, more texture than anything she was saying.

A tourist came in. A girl. Maybe a year younger than me. She was alone. I wondered if she'd come to escape her family. I told her the ticket was two pounds fifty and she turned around and went right out the door. Her thighs were white as flags of defeat.

M started speaking again. She said that the year before Leo was born F had stopped singing altogether. That he seemed so sad. And that she'd thought that perhaps Leo being born would make things better. But it hadn't. He sang but it wasn't the same. He had got worse when Leo was a toddler. Did worse mean his hands on her skin? She was wearing a blue button up shirt, the sleeves folded to her elbows and I was almost angry at her for showing those marks where anyone might see them. It would have been easy to unroll the sleeves.

That's why I always have to stick up for your brother, she said, *so he knows he's loved.* And I wanted to tell her that she had got it the wrong way around. That F took

175

care of me because she was never looking. That he was sad because she never saw us. I don't know now which came first. Did F resent Leo because M favoured him or did M favour Leo because F resented his son? There is no playback tape for family.

Briefly, I wondered if Leo was not F's son, perhaps he was Charlie's, perhaps that was why we'd come to live in this salt-licked town. I said, *Leo's his too* and waited for her to contradict me.

Yes, he is, she said. *Of course he is. But he's a boy. Fathers and sons . . . it's common. Your father's softer with you.*

And for a second, I wished my brother not dead but non-existent, a non-body who didn't need drama lessons or M's eyes or to be making rattle-clatter trouble. And then I felt guilty, because he was my brother and he'd once given me his tooth fairy money because he didn't need it.

I'm not going. God, it feels so strange to tell you about this time. Trying to summon the anger and the shake in my breath, I feel myself getting hot despite all the years that have passed.

Don't be ridiculous. M shifted her weight, left foot to right. *Go home, get your stuff, come meet me here.*

You can't make me. I thought of his song. The twisting, looping rise of it. And his face as he drank alone in the kitchen. And the way he had held me after I told him about Andrew. I thought of his animal God watching us both. I didn't know where the python in him came from, why he seemed to hold her too hard, why small things seemed to shake him so much.

I asked, *Why did you even marry him if you didn't like him? He needs us. We can't just leave him by himself.*

I keep seeing that past me, standing with her chest out, declaring that her father needed her. If she wasn't me, I'd find her ridiculous. We stood and M's face went very cool and flat, smooth as a sea pebble. I fiddled with my bracelet. It was woven from embroidery thread. I'd made it in school a few years before but this past year the thing had been to wear them ironically. The threads were very soft and I rubbed them between thumb and forefinger.

My mother wasn't fiddling with anything. She wasn't a fiddler. Nor did she sigh. But she splayed her fingers out very straight for a moment, so they almost bent backwards. M took a breath. *It was stupid. I thought if you didn't see . . . Children who see things. It's not good for them. There are studies. I thought I could . . . we could . . . control it. Help him. Portion it out. But that was stupid. I should have known better.*

I thought I'd get over things as I got older. I'd grow calm and fair and would see everyone with equanimity and sympathise with them each in turn. But writing this I can feel that teenage girl, not far below my skin. I've never understood why M didn't hoist me into the car right then. Why she didn't tell me to shut up and drag me along, the way she did when it was time to go to Leo's school plays. Was it tiredness? Was she too sore? Or did she really believe that little girl in her big jacket? I don't know.

I'm not going, I repeated.

The wind picked up. A wrapper chased down the street.

Kit, she said, *I can't make you.*

Where are you going? I asked.

177

I can't tell you, she said, weight shifting on her feet as if already preparing to walk away. *It wouldn't be fair. If you stay, you'd have to keep it a secret.*

I picked a paperclip up off the desk and began to unwind it.

If you need anything, you can ask Charlie, she said. *Call me if you change your mind.*

I thought of M who had Leo and Charlie and about F who had only music and me.

5

M aybe this is a form of cowardice, to write rather than to speak. Yesterday, when you were doing that thing where you make your left hand into a little man with two legs who struts up and down my stomach, I thought I might say it all. Then we walked to the cafe to get brown rice with little pink pickled radishes. And I couldn't.

I don't want our future to be dirtied by my past. But to have a real relationship, to have a chance, I think you have to share your stories. The big ones that make you you. Isn't that part of loving someone? I sidestepped this in those first heady weeks together, I told you other stories. Stories about wild parties and bad flatmates and the time a friend and I slept in Hampstead Heath overnight. Stories that made it seem like you knew me. Stories in which I made mistakes – but nothing like this.

I am so close to the end now. I don't want to write it. But I will. Even though I have spent so long trying not to think about what happened, it turns out that in writing, as in life, sometimes the sheer force of everything you've done keeps pushing you on.

Boat Days

I lay on my bed looking up at the painted eyes. They looked back at him. I wanted to tell him she'd return. But I didn't think that she would. Now the answer to *Who would you save if you could save anyone?* was simple. There were only two of us.

We should swap rooms, he said. Later, I would hear the exact same phrase from someone in a house-share trying to escape the smell of their ex. But I didn't know things like that back then. I only saw my father's long form in my thin bed. He was still wearing his shoes. The curved edges of the soles cutting into the fabric. Leo's bed was weirdly empty. The sheets never made. Sometimes I looked around expecting to see him but he was never there.

We swapped. I lay in their big bed, exactly where M had lain. It was harder to change the sheets in that larger bed. The duvet got tangled in its cover, so it lumped like a co-sleeper by my side and did not cover me.

We didn't need to switch beds. We could have slept like those sailors I'd read about in history class, who shared hammocks down in the hold. Me on the day shift and him on the night. He slept when the sun forced itself into our house. And at night, he played that song over and over and over again. Or spoke to God, his tone less that of prayer and more like someone leaving their twentieth answering phone message. I don't know if he had a medical-grade drinking problem. I don't think so. It seemed more as if he was a man who did not know what to do and was miming a man being sad. I missed my old nightmares which were never true in the morning. I used to let go of them as easily as a fist unclenching. But I could never do that while watching F.

Once he drank so much that he fell asleep on the hard kitchen chair. His head slumping forwards onto his chest. His body snail-shelling over itself. I worried he would choke. They'd told us about this in school. You can vomit in your throat and then choke on this vomit. I wasn't sure if this was true or one of those things they said to keep you from having fun. Not that F looked like he was having fun.

I went to my room and tried to wake myself up. I shouted in the body's ear. I slapped her face. But it was no more effective than the first time. I thought of the way sleeping feels like sinking and I told myself, *Up. Come up. Swim up. Rise up. Fly up. Wake up.*

I don't know how long I would have kept trying. There was a smashing sound and then I was in my body. And that body was going downstairs. And then that body was standing in the kitchen in her bare feet and on the ground the good glass had broken into diamonds. Each one glinting up at me.

Wake up, I told him then. He blinked at me, slow and steady. And then he threw up. Brown foam on pyjamas and the kitchen floor, the liquid no thicker than rock-pool water.

I helped him off with his shirt and prodded him upstairs to bed. Before he went back to sleep, he said, *Love you Sweetie.*

Without M

The mornings were quiet with only the sound of my feet. I wasn't Leo's age. I didn't need a mummy. But still I found myself counting out what she had left behind. A painting her father had done of a sad brown cow hung in our hallway. A vase that she said belonged to her mother, small and white. She'd put some marram grass in that vase and it had dried hard and crunchy. Most of her clothes still hung in the wardrobe in my parents' room. When I couldn't sleep, I ran my hands over them, and they rippled like the sea. I tried on her jackets but they pinched me in the shoulders and under the arms. Her cherrywood caddy of tea still sat on the counter next to the kettle. One morning, I knocked it over. The green fragments of sencha poured out. The caddy fell to the floor with a *thok*. I was alone in the kitchen at the time. I found it hard to move, looking at the green mess. The oddness that she would not come home and scold me reverberated strangely around my chest. I, like the house, seemed to have more space inside of me. Some fragments of tea had fallen on my bare feet and pushed their way between my toes.

I texted her, *Spilt your loose leaf. Sorry.*
Sencha?
Yes.
It's okay.

I swept up the leaves, badly. A few hours later she texted, *Are you okay?*

Yes.

Do you want to come with us?

Do you want to come home?

It was a non-museum day. I finished the rest of the tea and took the bread out of the freezer. M always sliced and froze the bread when it was going stale. I toasted two pieces and covered them in a thick layer of strawberry jam. I put out two plates and carried them both up to F.

He was lying in bed awake, looking towards the curtains, as if he could see through them.

Breakfast? I asked.

Thanks, Caterpillar.

I sat on the floor and ate my toast. I licked the jam from the corners of my mouth. We didn't talk for a bit. Then he said, *Have you heard from your mother?*

Yeah.

How is she?

Don't know.

Can you do me a favour?

Yes?

Could you bring me some water? My head is killing me.

I did. And when I came back he said, *Thank you.*

It was very hard. I made it myself from scratch.

For being here, Kitkat. Thank you.

I didn't have to travel far, I said.

He reached out and he held my hand softly for a long time.

Little Princess

In the years after I'd moved to the city but before I met you, I partied hard and was always making my way across the dark in the night bus. Often there were men who wanted to talk to me. I remember one in particular. I didn't really get a good look at him. He was more a shape than a person. I kept my eyes focused on the textured vinyl of the bus floor. An empty beer can rolled up and down under the seats with the motion of the bus. He started talking louder and louder as if volume was the problem. And then he stopped talking to me and started talking at me. *Daddy's little princess doesn't want to chat, does she?* Something like that. He kept saying it, *Daddy's little princess. Daddy's little princess.*

I wanted to run off the bus or maybe to vomit – I could feel it there in my throat. I held onto the ridge of my keys like I'd read you were supposed to. I imagined stabbing him in his little eyes.

All the time he was describing me. Describing how I was lonely. How I'd go home and fuck myself. *Daddy's little princess.*

I held the keys so tight that they got warm. But I stayed on until my stop, hurrying down the steps without looking at him.

The Edge of the Bed

One night, F stumbled into his own room. I was already there, playing a puzzle game on my phone. He fell down around me. His chest was against my back. His arm was around my shoulders. The smell of him lay like a blanket over both of us. A part of him moved slightly against my thigh. A soft pressure. Uncertain – like a hand that goes up and down in class. I knew what it was and tried not to know. His face was against my neck.

I would die for my family.

I know, F, I said. Hoping that my voice would remind him who I was.

I would die.

I attempted to roll a little, to create a gap between our bodies. But his arms pulled me back. His body felt hot. Some internal thermostat in overdrive. The pulsing against my leg continued. I reached and felt the curved ridge at the edge of the bed. I dug my fingertips into the side of the mattress. He wasn't moving his hips. It was just that one part of him, flexing.

My phone, now on the floor, lit with a text from Andrew. It vanished before I could read the words. I willed myself to sleep so that I could use my mind to walk right out of the room. F's arm was heavy over my body and then it wasn't and he was asleep.

When I finally slept, I left as fast as I could. Walking quickly and without purpose. Stopping only when our house had disappeared behind me. It had taken me a long time to sleep and most of the street was dark, only a few lonely TVs still telling their stories. I stopped and closed my eyes trying to empty myself of thoughts.

The sound of feet thumping through the dark caught my breath before I remembered that I had no body here. Nothing that could be hurt or taken advantage of. I was safe.

The shape approached – a jogger. I'd seen them before though rarely so late. Some with flashing fluorescent bands and others who flitted darkly, their only warning the rubber thud of their shoes. As the shape got closer, I recognised it in the town's pale light. Elise. Her hair pulled smooth around her skull. The legs that beat me on every lap now darting towards me. Did her parents know she was running alone in the dark? Did they care?

I didn't know how fast I could run without a body. As fast as thought? I turned and began to run, hearing her step behind mine – less a pursuer and more a relay partner. She levelled with me. For a while I matched her pace for pace. The town curving around us. I tried to watch her without slowing. To see in her shoulder or calves when she would turn. And I found that I could tell. We had barely spoken but our bodies were familiar.

She ran us inland and up the hill. Not slowing but building speed. Her Lycra-smoothed frame stroked my arm as she slipped past. I pushed to keep up. I had no lungs to ache and yet I could feel her outstripping me. The white-blonde of her hair a gleam now. The sharp points of her

189

elbows pushing back. Her limbs tucked close and tight, her body an arrow-slit silhouette in front of me. She seemed too perfect to live beyond the race – a girl made only to swim and to run and to flee. She'd go on to do comedy nights and collect funds for women's causes and feed her rescue whippets only the best kibble. She was more than speed, I just didn't know it then. Then we were two girls running through the dark. Eventually, she was out of view, following her own path through the labyrinth of our town.

When I woke up, F had rolled away from me. When he woke up, I fried bacon and eggs. I looked into F's eyes and then down at his feet in their old sheepskin slippers. I waited for him to say something and he didn't. He may never even have known anything happened.

Escape

After that I couldn't stay home. I needed to be out of there. Either F was asleep or he was talking. Telling stories about America and angels and things he'd heard politicians say on the radio. It wasn't clear if he was talking to me or to M or himself.

I walked. Not through houses. You can have too much of people. I walked along the cliff path, along the coast. I didn't see Elise again. Her route must have altered. I went further. Up through the car park at the edge of town, and then on past the camper vans that were lined up in a grid and surrounded by a pine fence, as if they were animals that might escape. Lace cut the light as it seeped through their windows. The moon caught on the sea and smashed into slivers. I walked in bare feet. If they had been flesh they would have bled, but they didn't. I only felt as if they might. Blood might have been a relief. I walked past moonlight and into milky morning. The gulls shouting out about the sun's arrival and the sound of animals in the dune grass skittering in or out of their holes. I walked so far that I hit the nearest village and saw the trucks arriving with supplies for the supermarkets, spilling out new-born bread.

But I woke up back home, without even a grain of sand between my toes.

A Kind Man

I don't know if Cassandra noticed a change in me in the weeks after M left. She was busy with her own things. Once I walked into her office and she was scrolling down the property listings for our town. Little houses piled on top of one another, as if a giant child-god had plucked them up and stacked them. She minimised the tab quickly. I laughed because I didn't care what she did.

This left a lot of time to text Andrew about nothing. Andrew was always fast to reply with a joke, a picture ripped from the bowels of the internet, or a silly drawing. I told him that M had left, though not why. He looked concerned and wrapped his hand around mine. I said that I'd decided to stay, that *it was my choice*.

We'd never talked about his dad not being around. It was just a fact, an absence. It felt impossible to bring up because if it wasn't okay then what would I say? I didn't know how to fold that into his sea-monster movie. I wondered if it would have been better, if M had left me with F when I was a baby. If it had always been the two of us, if she'd cut it cleanly. But she dawdled.

I'm glad you're still here, he said.

He kissed me for a long time. When a person kisses for that long are they drinking the other's carbon dioxide? Was that why I felt warm and dizzy?

Finally, I wrote to M, *Can you just come home?*

But she replied only to ask if I wanted to be picked up, to meet her and Leo. *F isn't okay without you,* I wrote. It took her a long time to reply to that, little dots rising and falling on screen. In the end, she asked me again to go with her and when I didn't reply she called, the phone vibrating loudly on the museum's desk. I let it buzz.

At lunch, I asked Cassandra, *If your family were all on a boat and they all fell off who would you rescue first?*

Whoever was closest, she said but I told her that wasn't a real answer.

My mother, she said. *Wouldn't everyone choose their mother?*

Before I could reply, she asked me why I was asking. When I explained that it was a game, a game everyone played, she told me it wasn't. That she didn't know anyone who played this game. We'd run out of the food that M had left in the house, and so the lunch I had brought was a packet of chocolate digestives and a banana. I was sucking the chocolate off the last digestive when Cassandra said, *I don't know. Actually, maybe my girlfriend? Is that bad?*

I laughed and asked if I could leave work early, not much, half an hour. I was tired of holding my face together in a way that looked normal. She agreed.

I turned right rather than left from the museum, taking the turn to Charlie's hotel. It was a tall Victorian beast built when our town had been more popular. The rich Victorians came down to promenade, to take the sea air and so on. The photographs of this time were the museum's greatest pride. The hotel's front was three different colours of brick: yellow, red and, in a few spots above the windows, purple-black. The windows were tall and high, to take in the sea. It seemed huge to me then, although I have since got lost in a conference hotel, winding down corridor after corridor of plywood and grey ceilings, and I suppose Charlie's hotel would look homey if I went back.

At the front desk was a girl whose name I didn't know but whose over-chewed lips I recognised. She was local. I made a half-nod in recognition of this fact. I'd never met anyone who stayed overnight but the bar and restaurant were where everyone's parents went for their anniversaries. The girl looked at me like I had no business being there.

Can I talk to Charlie, please? I wondered if I should have said Mr Stenson. I wondered if she'd think that I was Charlie's teenage fling.

She called him and told me to wait in the lobby. There was a large orchid in the middle of a table with two fat teardrop shaped leaves. My fingers itched a little looking at it. Part of me wanted to tear them off and see if it was plastic or plant. I didn't know exactly what I was going to tell Charlie, only that M needed to come home. It shouldn't, I thought, be possible to take a bag of laundry and leave your life.

It was the sort of hotel where the staff don't have uniforms but also they do. Each person wore a black T-shirt and jeans, though the T-shirts varied in cut and shape to give the illusion of difference. I watched their gold badges go by. When Charlie appeared, he too was wearing a variation of this outfit. I didn't know if he was in uniform or if he'd made all the staff dress to match him.

Hi Charlie.

Kit, how're you doing? He shaped his face into the expression of someone who gave a shit. And that annoyed me. He was leaning forward to emphasise that he really wanted to know.

Can you tell M to come home?

No, Kit, I can't do that. It wouldn't be healthy for your mother . . . for either of them.

I wanted to tell Charlie that he should go back to calling me Katherine and also what did he know of F's health? Charlie ushered me into his office, which was nothing like F's office. Here there was a big window that looked out onto the sea and plants growing in little tubs. A scent diffuser sat on a shelf next to matching ring-binders. He asked if F was hurting me. He said the word *hurting* softly, as if volume itself might bruise me. I shook my head, in short sharp shakes, the way I'd seen dogs whisk off sea water. I didn't want to be talking to Charlie.

M had taken so little. It wasn't enough to start a life with.

Do you want to speak to your mother?

I'm not the one who needs her. She should call him, at least, talk to him.

Charlie reached into his pocket and, for a moment, I thought he was going to call her and that she would appear. He removed a wallet, the thick leather kind that men in movies have. He took out three notes with the Queen's face repeating in purple on each one.

Reiko was worried that . . . he paused.

It was true that we didn't have any groceries. I hadn't asked F for money and he hadn't gone out. But he'd made pasta a few times with tomatoes from a can. True, his spices were off. He'd been a good cook. Now his attention wasn't in it. Too much salt and then not enough and then so much garlic powder that I stood back from Cassandra the next day. F didn't eat, moving the food around the plate like I'd seen girls at school do.

The notes looked slippery in Charlie's hand. And I wanted to take them because when you are young, you always want to take money. It represents a rare freedom. I shook my head. I had too much pride. Charlie put the notes down on my knee, his movement careful, his fingers never touching me.

He cares about us, I said. *He's a kind man.*

Kit, what can I do to help you?

Why didn't you ever get married?

Kit, I'm only forty. I know that seems old to you but a lot of people aren't married in their forties.

Is it because of M?

Charlie smiled, the sort of smile people gave Leo when he talked about growing up to be a famous actor. The smile you give the very stupid. *Is that what you think?* He asked. *No. Kit. She's my friend. I want her to be safe. I want you to be safe. Your father is not . . . What he did is not kind.*

Are the orchids real?

Give me your phone, Kit. And I did because I hadn't yet learnt that someone being older than you didn't make them your boss. I even unlocked it for him. As I passed him the phone, the notes fell to the floor, one after the other. He put in his number.

Call me if you need anything. Anything at all. And then he stood up, which meant that I stood up and then I knew that my time was over.

Twins

I plunged into being with Andrew, spending every non-museum day with him. We stayed at his house – his mother was rarely in. After sex, we lay looking at each other and his breath tasted sweet and sour like orange juice and waking up, and he ran his hands slow, slow, slow along my ribcage. I sank down into the mattress and let myself be measured by his fingers. I looked into his eyes and at the lashes gathered in clumps like his thinnest brushes. I moved to touch a lash and he pulled back.

Sorry, I said.

Don't blind me.

I just wanted to feel them. And I pulled his hands back down, pulling the weight of him on top of me. *I feel more real with you here.*

I could feel his body against my body. You once asked me how I could bear to be with a man. But to me he didn't feel like a man or even a boy. He was all texture and warmth. The hairs on his legs curled against my calves. What I liked most were his eyes, the way that he was always looking at me.

They're not the same, his hands were on my ribs. I didn't understand. So he showed me. Again, his hand traced the curve of each side of my ribcage. He was right – one curved more while the other was slightly taller. There were twins in my year, identical and yet not, there were small differences in height, in softness of cheeks. Our biology teacher said it meant one of them had got more nourishment in the womb, though I'd seen them eat at lunch and it was the smaller sister who was always the hungrier, stealing the sandwich crusts her sister left. I looked down at my ribs – my own uneven twins, two shadowed hills.

Scoliosis is what this twist of the spine is called – it pushes your ribs out of alignment. Mine was mild. Andrew was the first person to find it. When I think of it now, I still feel the heat of his two palms. I curled against him feeling soft and seen.

Then I went home. I rinsed each of F's bottles to put them in the recycling. The palest of golds poured into our old white sink. He was in the kitchen then, writing by hand in his small notebook.

He said, *When I was young, my mom used to stick Bible verses up on the fridge.*

Uh-huh. I cut the metal rings off the bottle necks as you were supposed to.

She'd make us memorise them. She did it even before I could read. I used to think everything written down was written by God. Funny, right?

Then he showed me. The piece of paper. It was a song by a band he liked. All about joy and strength. His handwriting tumbled over the lines. He stuck it to the fridge with one of Leo's alphabet magnets.

Okay

I texted M – *Meet me at the pool.*

In the summer most of the swim team swam in the sea. Our hopes weren't national – to win against each other or to beat our own records was enough. In the afternoon, the pool filled up with the public but it was reasonably empty in the mornings. It was not a place that M would be seen.

Swimming pools, like churches, have their own sonics. The echo doubles your steps and doubles each lap of the water against the poolside. The swimming cap circled my scalp, pressing down as if trying to cut off blood to my brain, so that more of it might go to my legs. I got in. The smell of rubber dissolved into disinfected blue. The ventilation panted above me.

I know you don't like the way swimming frizzes your hair. But I've always enjoyed that permeation. A person swims in the water but the water swims in them too. There is no word for being in the air, in the way that being in the water is called wet. But there is a feeling of breaking into that air, eyes all misted, and looking and looking for the person you want to see you win. She was always at my matches.

Her dark hair always gleamed in the pool lights and her body would angle forward, her chin jutting. F would be there too sometimes, leaning on the railings and looking down at us all, cheering in a wild, erratic way. Shouting *Caterpillar* and *Kitkitkitkit*. But he loved everything I did. M's focus was different, the way she looked at me, it was not as if she wanted me to win but as if she were keeping me buoyant using only her will.

I did a lap.

And another.

Another.

Another.

Another.

Another.

Another.

At each end of the pool, I did a turn in which my body spun sideways. My eyes flinging themselves towards orange and white bleachers.

Another.

Another.

Another.

Another.

I had sometimes wished it was possible to race naked and not end up with red streaks on my thighs and shoulders as my suit failed to turn with my body. I felt the elastic bite.

Another.

Another.

Another.

Water in the throat burns. That was why I never took up smoking. The water burn was better.

Another.

Another.

Another.

An obliteration that was different from sleep. The obliteration of movement.

Another.

Another.

Another.

Once I read about Japanese pearl divers, women who were called Ama or sea women. Women who threw themselves down. Once I fantasised that some great-great-great-grandma of mine was a sea woman. But I was descended from people who went across and not down. Across, across, and over.

Another.

Another.

Another.

Another.

And then she was there. In the bleachers with her nylon bag and her hair shiny as a rock above the waves. Her eyes followed me along the water, the place where she always seemed to see me most clearly.

I swam another.

After a race we pulled ourselves by our arms out of the pool. But now I paddled to the ladder. I took it slowly. My toes monkey-gripped the steel.

I looked at her with that bag held in front of her like a shield.

How is he? she asked.

He needs you.

A tall stranger opened the men's changing room door and the pool filled with the creak.

No, he doesn't, she said. *He needs to see someone. But not me. I already stayed longer than I should have. Divorce is hard on children.* She spoke as if she were referring to abstract children. She seemed to avoid looking at me. *But, it's not the worst thing. Kit. I'm sorry. I don't know why I thought I could keep it from you.*

I noticed that she wasn't wearing any make up, and her lips looked wilted. Had she kept it from me? Or had I known? Had knowing and not knowing been what opened my mind? Maybe.

I need you to come home, I put the emphasis on the *I,* as if by stretching it out I was making myself so large that I would be impossible to overlook.

Okay, she held the edge of her bag tightly.

Okay? Something in me staggered like I'd charged a door that wasn't locked.

Okay, if you need me. Go get dry or you'll get a cold.

In the changing room I took off my swimming costume, balled it into a plastic bag, rinsed the chlorine out of my hair, patted myself dryish, pulled on the clinging normality of my clothes, emptied my bladder, picked at a hang nail. I pictured walking home with M and her seeing the mess of our house. Of us – me and F. I knew that if I didn't get off the seat then she would come looking for me. I cried a bit. A hot sort of thing. And when it was done, I knew I would undo my request. I don't know how to explain but I was sure that I couldn't ask her to come back.

I'm glad. I'm grateful that that past self, with her goose-pimpled thighs and aching shoulders, knew that much. I'm sad that we did not have the sort of relationship other girls have with their mothers. I over or underestimated her, I think now. But I know this was the right thing.

M was waiting for me by the steady glow of the vending machines.

You don't have to come home, I said.

She nodded like when I was small and I pointed out *Bird, car, dog.* Right answer.

Come with us. She handed me a cold coke, like she always did, knowing that I liked sugar after moving. The fizz hopped in my throat.

I'm fine, I said.

I'll come get you if you need me to.

Mmm. I had a wish. An absurd wish that F could shrink, could go backwards and backwards in time, like in that movie, getting younger and younger. I wished he was a little boy no older than Leo and that we might all fit together into the back of M's car.

I'm at Charlie's hotel. He, Charlie, thinks we should leave. He's trying to find us a good place, not here. Out of town. He thinks it would be better. But I told him I needed to stay close to you.

I wondered why he hadn't brought her down to meet me. They were so close and yet I hadn't seen Leo around town. Were they hiding in that small room all day? Staying close for me?

Really, I'm fine, I said.

A harried looking family ran past us, all water wings and dancing goggles. M looked at me and I looked at her.

You leave first, I said. *I'll be okay.*

A Call

A day later, F got a call from the organisers of the Sun Songs. I hadn't even known someone organised it. I assumed the musicians appeared the same way that terns migrate for the summer on their grey wings, all knowing where to be, without discussion. I couldn't hear the other side of the call speak. I only saw the way his face moved.

Do you remember when we went to the Natural History Museum and I couldn't stop looking at the skeletons when you wanted to go see the butterflies and you accused me of being morbid? I didn't want to seem weird back then. Too late for that now. The reason I was staring is that I'm still amazed how the skull accommodates so many subtle shifts, so many hieroglyphics of emotion.

The exact movements in F's face were slight. Maybe something around the eyes or edges of his mouth, maybe even in the place where his ear met his skull. But I knew it was not a good call. I guessed it was M telling him again that she wasn't coming back. Or maybe a client asking why no work had been done.

I listened while pretending not to listen. With a sharpie I drew a band of eyes around my wrist.

Mmm.

Why?

It's only two weeks away.

You can't.

It's not fair to the others.

Fine. Okay. I'll tell them that.

He went to the bookshelf and took down the bottle of whisky. He poured himself a drink. It was still early, the sun high and gold as the dram. Out the window the apricot tree had put out pale new leaves. Flies hovered around the sink, even though he used to be the one to do the washing up. He wore the same shirt again and again – a lavender-blue that might once have been darker.

Who was that? I asked.

He told me it was the organisers calling to tell him that his set had been cancelled. I told him there would be another year. But he shook his head. There had been *rumours* and *gossip* and he was *out*. With each word he took a drink.

A fly settled on the table and I hit it with the palm of my hand. It left a tiny brown squelch on my skin. He blinked at me. I washed my hands with Fairy Liquid.

Charlie, I said, *It was probably Charlie.*

F made a face like I'd tried to make him eat that fly.

I thought of what M had said about how maybe we could all move elsewhere. How F might have been happier somewhere else, better. If I had kept my mouth shut, it might have happened. If I'd acted with greater subtlety. If I'd taken my little brother's hand and chosen the correct moment to walk out of the room, to tell him that the adults were only arguing the way he did with his friends at school. That it would all be over by lunch break. If I hadn't let M see that Leo was scared.

We could move, I said. *Somewhere else. America.*

No, he said, *This is our home. They're not going to make us leave.*

Okay, I said. *I'm sorry.* It felt impossible that we might spend two more years, alone together, in that house. Me sleeping in his bed and he in mine, like dolls thrown back into a dollhouse all out of order. Me watching his one-man show.

We're out of milk, I added, *Do you want me to pick some up?*

Thanks Caterpillar, that would be great.

I waited for him to say that he had some work to do, so that I could get up and walk over to Andrew's to have sex and watch cartoons.

It was a good song, you know, probably my best, he said.

I'm sorry.

It's not your fault.

I know.

His hand drummed the edge of the table. I knew that expression. His knuckles knocked fast up and down on the pine and I tried to hear a rhythm but there was only the sound of wood and bone.

F?

Don't.

He closed his eyes, and he pulled his lips together. His face pinked. His neck went white as bone, as God's dove, as a squirt of suntan lotion. Every metaphor I write is wrong. It was like nothing. There was no art to the moment.

I always skip over the tense sections in movies. You laugh at me. But I can't help it. I can cope with a rain of bullets. Someone swinging at someone else with a katana, fine. Great. What gets me is the heaviness of the air. The way everything seems like a sign. Can I skip here? Fast-forward? Jump?

Don't, he said.

It was a good song.

I know. Kit, just go. Get the milk.

They're idiots.

It's fine, Kit.

I touched his shoulder and he pushed my hand away. He picked up the whisky bottle by the neck, to pour himself another finger.

You could play it for me?

What was I thinking? Perhaps I was trying to be the anti-M. Someone who was open from every pore. That if he could see it, it would calm him.

Kit. Could you be quiet? He held the bottle up as if it were a plea. His fist going tight, his knuckles white. *I need to think.*

I—

His arm going back. A sound. My eyes jamming shut. The floor was wet. F's hand was empty.

Shit. In F's voice.

His body close to mine. The whole room smelt of him.

Stay still, he said. And I did like a trained dog even though I didn't know why.

What had happened, I see in panels. Like something Andrew would have drawn.

Panel 1: Bottle hits wall.

Panel 2: A smash.

Panel 3: Triangles of glass fly.

Panel 4: From above, my hair toothed with glass.

It isn't really a memory. More of a reconstruction. At the time what I saw was: My father's neck now a normal colour. His chin. Also a feeling of his hands moving slowly through my hair. Gently, pulling on strands the way you see gulls sometimes pulling out the down of their chicks.

He put each shard on the table. They caught the light the way engagement rings do in advertisements. So many colours. I wondered how long before everything in that house smashed.

When he was done, he said, *There.* And, *Arms up.*

I raised my arms.

He picked me up. It had been so long since he carried me, not for years. But there we were. He sort of swung around on the spot. For a moment, I hung in the air. His hands cupping the sides of my ribs. My feet felt heavy. They gave a little clunk when he put me down in a dry spot. He turned my jaw left and right. Up and down.

Your face is okay, he said.

And when I didn't reply he said, *I'm sorry Kit. This isn't me.*

Should I get the milk? I asked.

Don't go. He held me on his lap, his fingers running through my hair though there was nothing there. A wasp flew in through the window and landed on the puddle. And in silence together we watched it drink. In my head I tried speaking to his God. Not praying, but asking, Why is he like this? What is it in him that does this? Could you extract it like a tonsil? We don't need it.

I'm sorry, Caterpillar. I don't want this. I'm not this. I love you so much.

Later, in my parents' room, I found that the top of my left foot had been nicked. A thin red-brown *S* ran down to my little toe.

Sea View

O ne night, I decided to go to the hotel. Spirit-body climbing the service stairway. Poking my head through door after door. I was no longer surprised by the fucking or the Netflix or the snoring or the people lying in the dark, spot-lit by their phones. The unsleeping rooms were better because I knew immediately that they were not my family. In the dark rooms, I had to stand over each bed, each woman's mess of hair, and ask, *Is it you?*

I found them eventually. In the biggest room, the lights off but the curtains open and the sea crashing outside. There was one bed, large and canopied with filmy gauze, the sort of bed you'd put Sleeping Beauty in, not a middle-aged therapist and her child. I didn't think of them as that yet, I don't think I ever have. I'm simply trying for objectivity.

M curled around Leo. They were so complete in that bed – mother and son. Later, I'd read that Jesus had sisters, but I'd never seen these girls in paintings. It's never Jesus playing with the goats while his sisters wrap their hands around Mary's. You don't see that. Perhaps that's why my brain knew to read the scene as whole, not lacking any element.

They looked so peaceful and so safe and who was I to ruin that?

Leo is famous now. If I showed you his face, you'd recognise it. He doesn't act but you'll have seen him stripped down to his underwear on the sides of buses. He was beautiful but not a talented enough liar. In interviews, he doesn't often talk about his family. But when he does it is always M. I want to ask him if he remembers that hotel, and what it felt like, and if he noticed that the sound of the sea was louder here than it was at home. But Leo and I don't talk much.

Better

That next week F was better. He cleaned the floor. He bought broccoli. He didn't sing. He drank water and coffee. He opened the bills. He washed my clothes and folded them. He bought the milk. He cried only at night, biting down on his fist. I believed he was sorry. He made me sandwiches from seeded bread to take to work. We didn't talk about Sun Songs. Better.

The cut on my foot didn't heal, but only because I picked at it. Pulling the brown scab up calmed me. Like plunging myself underwater, it steadied me in this body.

Sun Song

A week before Sun Songs, Cassandra printed a pile of worksheets. She used special yellow paper. When she handed me the sheets, her nails were adorned with small gold suns. She told me to give them to the children who came in.

I scanned them. There were supposedly 'fun' facts like –

August is hotter than June. This is called Seasonal Lag. It takes time for the world to heat up.

When we have our summer the people in the Southern Hemisphere have their winter.

Over one million Planet Earths could fit inside the sun.

There was a sun for them to colour in, though the paper was already yellow, so I didn't know what they were supposed to do. Burning red? Black solar eclipse?

Every year, people go to Stonehenge for the solstice, Cassandra said. *Fun fact!*

Seems pointless, I said. I preferred to see beautiful things online, where they were perfectly lit and framed, not in the scrum of living. We'd been to Stonehenge on a school trip a few years ago and I'd overheard Lia in the toilets calling me a stuck-up bitch.

They used to have a music festival there, you know. Until it was broken up by the police. Before you were born, she added.

214

Okay.

I was talking to Charlie, and he was thinking that maybe the Sun Songs could be bigger. A last hurrah of the summer festival, there's space for that.

I'm not sure anyone wants it to be bigger. Also, I don't know that people feel great about the earth being hotter.

Outreach, she said. *People would know about this place. It's beautiful.*

It's fine, I said.

Cheer up. It's summer. She offered me a piece of gum and I took it, revelling in the crack as my teeth pierced the sugary shell.

I didn't tell F about Charlie's music festival idea. Though I searched the old Stonehenge one and learnt the people fighting to keep it going included the *Mother Earth Circle*, *Devotees of the Sun Temple* and *The Magical Earth Dragon Society*. I was jealous in a way. I wished I had the self-confidence of someone who could go around calling myself a member of *The Magical Earth Dragon Society* and not care if they got spat at. I texted Andrew about them and he told me that he'd found an article that said some of the druids used to ejaculate onto the earth at dawn.

Disgusting, I wrote.

I know
They'll do it in the sea next
Probably already do
Disgusting!

Two days before the Sun Songs, F was working at his computer again. It appeared that he had finished the parade of sadness. I asked how it was going and he said, *Late but most of these people are morons. They don't know how long anything should take. Don't worry so much, Kitkat.* He was in a good silly mood. I asked if I could have Andrew over for dinner, festival night. Though I didn't say the festival night, I said *in two days.*

F paused, doing some calculation. He looked out the window, not at the apricot tree but past it, to the row of houses behind. And I scolded myself for not letting the good moment simmer on. Then he asked, *Does Andrew like vongole?*

Anything with an Italian name always feels fancy to me, even though this was just clam pasta and clams were common where we lived. The afternoon of the Sun Songs, F and I went together down to the market stand where you could buy fresh fish.

We walked past the spot on the shore where they were setting up for the Sun Songs. Someone had laid out a stage. Not a huge one. Charlie's dream had not yet come true and the bands playing would be mostly local. The only exception was a band who'd had a single hit twenty years before and who were taking the train down from the city. But I thought this stage was a little bigger than in years past. Floodlights were lined up, like a row of cannons pointed at the stage. I tried not to look at it as we went past. I talked high and fast about the vongole and what else we needed. F looked at the stage and there was the familiar stillness of his anger – the way it seemed to pull him into himself.

At the stand, we bought a bag of clams. They clattered as we walked back up the hill. We strode quickly so they wouldn't get warm. I watched his face, carefully. He appeared calm. At home, we soaked them in salted water to make them clean themselves of grit. After the soak, F showed me carefully how to check if each one was alive. You must look for the clams that are slightly open, a little peep. Tap them with a finger or fork. The living ones close right up. Anything already closed or anything that remains open is dead. Life is the ability to change position.

When we knew they were alive, we shucked them, tearing their sweet orange bodies from the shells. We did all but five, which we left in their shells for show. I'm sorry that I've never made vongole for you.

As he was peeling garlic, he asked, *Do you know if your mother is still in town?*

He said it without looking at me, casually.

I denied this. For her sake or his or mine I don't know.

She should have told you. He sprinkled salt on the side of the garlic. *You shouldn't leave your child.*

I'm fine. I made a big smile to show how fine I was.

He pressed down on the clove with the flat of a wide knife, crushing it.

Andrew arrived exactly on time. He must have been standing on the pavement outside, timing it, in order to be so precise. I liked that about him. He hadn't dressed up, but his hair was brushed carefully to one side and his hands were uninked, not even at the edges of the nails. As if announcing him, the music came up from the shore, amplified enough to travel all the way here. Though by the time it arrived, it was a malignant whisper.

217

F looked up from the pot as I ushered Andrew into the kitchen. When I saw F's eyes, I knew he had heard the music. I had the urge to tell Andrew, no, no, no, this isn't about you. But then F slid on a welcoming face. I suggested we put on a record. Our music was only quiet, but at a closeness that might protect us.

With a flourish, F apportioned the pasta, the long yellow strands dripping with olive oil. With Andrew's body, the table felt fuller. F moved a chair around to sit at the head and we sat on either side. He drank the wine that he'd used to make the pasta sauce and I felt grand and European. It felt like the food of places where people ate outside among ruins in long floating dresses.

We talked of normal things. About school and work and the news and no one mentioned M or Leo and F tapped his feet along to the record player. Andrew's foot brushed my shin under the table and I smiled at him.

F asked him about his comic and Andrew said that he'd had an idea for a new one in which I might be the star. Or a version of me. I nudged his foot harder. I hadn't heard of this.

You like her then? F asked. Half the bottle of wine was gone.

Andrew moved a clam shell to the edge of the plate. It clicked as it rocked against the china.

Leave him alone, I said.

As Andrew replied, *Yes.*

Good, said F.

There was a pause in which no one knew exactly what to say and I twirled spaghetti with my fork. Then Andrew, with a borrowed adult voice, asked F what he was reading at the moment. The answer was a book of saints. For a while they talked about this.

You know, Saint Catherine, they put her on a wheel and tore her apart piece by piece. Sometimes in paintings they have her hold a little wheel. Grim isn't it?

Why? Andrew asked his voice full of amazed horror.

They were into shapes. It's not all straight up and down crosses. They nailed Saint Andrew to a cross in the shape of the letter X.

As F spoke his voice was fat with awe. That God would speak to you, teach you miracles, love you, and let this happen. When he spoke about it, it was almost like when he sang, as if he was being lifted by a melody.

Andrew nodded along, not even flinching when F described the nails in Saint Andrew's hands. I've never been able to discover the exact branch of religion that F's people believed. It was too local, too particular to its time and place. I don't know if he found the saints there or elsewhere.

As he talked, F was buzzy and energetic. His face clear and full of purpose as it was sometimes, when he had an idea. He was always getting up to offer Andrew more water or ask if we wanted salt.

All the while, I could hear the music coming up from the sea, billowing towards us, getting gradually louder. And it wasn't long before the spaghetti was finished, leaving gleaming smears on our plates.

A sneak of dread wiggled in my chest that soon F and I would be alone in the house again. I told myself that as soon as I was asleep, I would follow Andrew back to his house. I wanted to lie next to him in his luxurious,

219

only-child double-bed. I wanted to feel the weight of his body and his arms nearby. I was thinking this when F said, *Why don't we go down to the beach? See how it's going.*

But, I said and did not finish. Because I couldn't say, but they don't want you. They told you they don't want you. What if Charlie had brought M and Leo under his great wing?

Andrew smiled and nodded. He knew and didn't know what was wrong. Knew that F's show was cancelled but I'd let him believe that the band had a falling out. Bands did that sort of thing.

They won't be any good, I said, and *I bet if you put a record on, we wouldn't even hear them.*

Don't fuss so much, Caterpillar.

I felt myself flush and F said, *Sorry should I not, not call you that in company?*

It took me a moment to understand that *that* was *Caterpillar* and *company* was Andrew. I was too busy playing through all the ways that going down to the beach might go.

F was already standing. He took a beer from the fridge and offered one to me and one to Andrew. Andrew looked at me, in his eyes a question. It wasn't that unusual for parents in our town to let their children have a beer. But this was the first time F had offered me a whole can of my own. I took it. And so did Andrew. The tin was cold and it foamed as I cracked it open. I held my mouth over the bubbles and the cloud rose against the top of my mouth.

As we left, Andrew reached out and took my free hand. I let my fingers be cradled in his for a step or two before letting go. It felt too strange to do it in front of F. I shoved my hand into my pocket as if it was cold, though it was a warm enough night.

F walked in front of us in long strides. Closer to the shore, the sound piled up. The beach was not the main beach, it was a strip a little to the west of the town centre. You had to walk through a car park and then down a steep flight of steps to the sea. The car park was full which meant that it was not just locals but people from the other towns filling the beach, though I could have told you that from the sheer number of bodies down by the sea. The beach was clogged with a crowd three or four times the size of our school. That's still how I think of crowds, perhaps because seeing us all laid out neatly in rows for assembly was the last time I had any grip on a number of people that large. I have always found it easier to think of people in twos and threes. The three of us walked down the steps to the sea. F first, then me, then Andrew. The metal handrail was cool under my palm, even though it must recently have been clutched by so many song-goers. The beer still balanced in my hand. I'd only made it half-way through.

The stage glowed. The music drowned out even the sea which was lying low and deceptively still. I wondered whether the fat brown seals, who could sometimes be found in this cove, were sleeping in secret sea caves or listening to us deep underwater. It helped to think about these things because then I wasn't staring too carefully at the back of F's neck and wasn't looking too closely at his hand on the rail. I could hear Andrew's steps behind my own, as if we were one person walking at double speed. But F moved almost silently. That worried me in a vague

221

way. I can analyse it now. I can say that too much care felt like a bad sign. If he had been happy, his feet would have clattered as they went. But when we reached the bottom and he turned to check us, his face looked smiling and relaxed. Tipsy perhaps, but not the drunkenness of an abandoned man. More like the way the boys I knew got, going out with their friends laughing as they chased each other up and down the street on their bicycles.

The crowd surrounded the stage in a shell formation that from a distance looked dense. As we got closer, it was easy to see gaps between the groups. Shoals of girls bunched tightly together. Couples clutched hands. I think I was the only person there with father and boyfriend and I felt that sharp sense of shame that they taught so well in school. I realised that I had, without thinking about it, put on my suede boots. I could already see there would be dark patches the next day.

F wound closer to the stage and we followed him. May, who sat to Andrew's right in history, shouted, *Hi!* We waved back. No one danced exactly, but the crowd swayed. People raised their phones to the sky, to take pictures or show they were there. Off to one side, someone was laughing, high and ridiculous. And the familiar waft of weed muscled through the salt air.

No one knew the words to the music. People weren't really here for these bands but for the crowd itself. I could see Lia and a girl I knew only vaguely kissing each other, and I wondered when that had happened. They looked at each other with a gentle focus that made them appear completely alone. Advertisements for beer and for sportswear flapped from above the stage. I tried to remember if they'd been there previous years. Maybe they had but I'd been too taken up with the music to notice.

I could hear F asking Andrew what sort of music he liked and Andrew replying. His taste in music was fine, nothing that obscure. It pleased F to suggest better, lesser-known artists, I could tell. I finished my beer, but there was nowhere to put it, so I held onto it like a baby with a rattle. At some point some girls I knew percolated near us, and I made a gentle grimace to acknowledge my father. They offered me a new drink. They'd come prepared. I took it because F was not really watching me, but listening to the music with his eyes shut. This was a sweet strawberry-lemonade thing with a sharp burn of vodka at the end. I don't think Andrew took one. Sometime later, he put his long arm around me and I leant into him. And I was grateful that he was here with me and F and that he wasn't ashamed to be seen with an old guy in a denim jacket that clattered with pins from concerts long forgotten by everyone but him.

I thought I saw Cassandra close to the stage, but I couldn't be sure. I didn't see M or Leo. By the time we'd arrived all the kids Leo's age had been scooped off to bed anyway. I felt myself beginning to relax.

And then Charlie came on stage.

Charlie looked taller up there. He took the microphone and he thanked us all for coming out. For supporting the community. For celebrating music and love and sunshine. He reminded us to clear up after ourselves and told us there were bins to the right of the stage and also in the car park. He told us that the music was over, but that for one night only the council had said it was okay if we wanted to stay on the beach. But please don't camp too near the water *as tides do rise*. He paused to indicate a joke. And somebody laughed. It was odd to think that if M had not stopped for pie, she might have ended up married to this man. This man standing high above us all, as if we were at a rally to celebrate him. That she might have had a daughter who was half Charlie, who stayed up with him in the night and who knew how he smelt – air conditioner? Carpet? Hotel soap? That she might still have a daughter with Charlie. She was not that old. It was possible. And then I said, *Why?*

I said it loudly, my voice having adjusted to the volume of the music and now there was only Charlie. Andrew and F turned to look at me. And my mouth kept going and I asked those questions that you're not supposed to ask.

Why? Why did you do it? I was looking straight at F tilting my chin up.

It? he asked.

M, I said. I could feel myself teetering. I don't think it was the beer or the strawberry drink. It might have been the sea which was sending wave after wave, as if applauding. I wanted to say *hurt*, I could feel the *r* at the top of my mouth.

F was staring at me. His face turned a pinkish-red. And then I began to hum his song, high and hard. The tempo was off. But I knew he could hear it. And then I stopped. It wasn't silent. There were far too many people for silence, but I didn't care about those people.

What about her? he said. And I could tell that the words were getting harder for him to spit out.

How could you do those things? And then her arm?
I didn't do anything to her arm.
And her neck. And her hand.
What?

I took F's hand. And I squeezed and I squeezed. I felt the fingers shift under me. *I saw you,* I said. And he was quiet. Very quiet. I could see the switch in him. I could see it buzzing behind his eyes. He tried to pull his hand from my grip and I held on.

Why? I asked. Though I think I knew then or it felt like I knew – what it was to love someone and hate them and want to crush them and want them to crush you.

Why? I said again through my teeth.

Stop it, he said. But I didn't. He took my arm with his free hand and started to yank it away. But I held on as tightly as I could. Heat jumped up through my squeezing hand. I didn't even care that his other hand was twisting the skin of my upper arm, or that I could feel my muscle and fat and arteries compressing under that hand.

Then he yanked and his hand broke free. My palm was sweat-sticky. He was still holding onto my arm, which now hung limply and without purpose.

Let go, I said. His T-shirt had ridden up a bit and I could see the pale band of father flesh at the stomach. We looked ridiculous. I had a vague memory of being dragged by my arm once before. My eyes blind with tears mid-tantrum, feet kicking pavement. Was it M or F doing the dragging then? I don't know but the sensation came back to me clear and hot. F did not let go.

And then I heard Andrew's voice.

Kit? Are you okay?

I had forgotten about him. I looked around. Bodies who might be classmates were close enough to hear, but my eyes were stinging and their faces blurred into unfamiliarity. The stage had gone dark. The compression in my arm sent a vague pain up my shoulder.

I'm fine, I said.

You're drunk, F said.

I'm not.

Andrew wasn't a hero. He was a boy who wrote about heroes. He would grow into a man who told stories about heroes and kingdoms and mermaids. I should have kept him separate. But there he was and he was saying that maybe F should let go of me.

I am talking to my daughter, F said.

Andrew rubbed the back of his neck. His hands seemed confused without anything to hold onto. I wanted to give him a pencil and say this is just a pose. I wondered if he would draw it later, me and F, the knotting of our arms. I thought that if I spoke carefully, kindly, to F this would be over. That he would let go. That we would go home. He was scared. I could feel it through his palm's heat. There are people who go to therapy to find out their parents were frightened little children inside. But standing on that loud beach, I understood that F was not a child or a man but simply an animal, a creature lock-jawed with fear. I was not afraid. I wasn't. Not of upsetting him. Just of going home and hearing him breathing so close for so many nights.

I think you should let go of her, Andrew said. And he stepped towards us. He put his hand on F's hand, trying to free me. We looked comical, I am sure – F's hand on me,

Andrew's hand on F's hand, as if we were executing some secret handshake. Their two bodies blocked my vision of anyone who might be watching us. The lights caught the edges of Andrew's hair which the wind had un-brushed and it stood up ridiculously.

Go away, Andrew, I said.

Kit.

Fuck off, I said. I said it clear and harsh. Because I didn't want him to be part of this matryoshka doll. I told him that it was none of his business. That I didn't want him there. That I wasn't some maiden on the rocks who needed rescuing. Or at least, that is what I think I said. I don't know. I know that when I was done, I said, *Go.* And he did. It was as easy as that. He looked over his shoulder once. His face small and confused.

F let go of my arm. I prodded where he'd held me, feeling the ache of it.

Better now? I asked.

Kit.

Can everyone stop saying my name?

F made a shape with his face, as if he was trying to rearrange himself into a father. But I couldn't wait. I didn't wait. I couldn't run through walls and I couldn't fly. But this body could move and I moved it. Running up along the sand. Past people who I might have known but who I registered only as bodies. I ran clumsily, the sand kicking up under my feet and seeping into those boots. I wasn't holding my drinks anymore. Maybe they were swallowed up by the sea. Maybe they found their way to the North Atlantic garbage patch. I don't know. This isn't a story about how I was good. I felt the heat of a cigarette brush my elbow as I ran past, too fast for a burn but enough that I felt its bite. And then I was going up up up the cliff steps. Lungs beating hard in my chest. Legs sore. Up and up. Each step slower than the last. Eventually, I slammed into someone's back. A green jacket.

Cunt, they hissed as I apologised. My breath came sore. I didn't know where I was running. Not to Andrew and not to Charlie and not to my home. From far below, I could hear someone shouting my name. I needed to sleep. I needed to dream myself somewhere else. But all I had was a car park.

Below

The car park was full. Vehicles stood flank to flank, like a herd of cattle looking out towards the water. I could see the shadowy bodies and, somewhere off to the edge, the brief bloom of sparklers. The stage lights were still up, the crew dismantling the set piece by piece like ants taking apart a dead moth. My hands jittered in my pockets. I wished I was one of the girls who smoked because then I would have something to hold.

I eeled between the cars because I could hear steps fast behind me. Around the border of the parking spaces was a little wooden fence, lower than my knees – as if that would keep any determined person from diving off the cliff. On the other side of the fence was grass, tufty with dandelions. This was my town and I knew it in the dark and in the light. And my feet had become night-footed. My brain had learnt how to unpick shadows. I knew that the edge was two strides beyond the fence, that there was room for me to tuck myself between the fence and the drop quite safely.

I huddled with my back to the fence and accordioned my knees. I could hear him shouting my name. Was it cruel to be hiding? His throat must hurt. I didn't move. Weeds scratched my skin. Someone was getting into their car, I heard it start and saw the yellow shapes catch on the metal flashing they used to hold the low fence together. Other cars blinked as the headlamps of this one caught their reflectors.

Kit, F shouted. *Kit?*

I pressed my chin into my knees and closed my eyes like a baby playing peekaboo. I didn't see him see me. But his feet picked up speed and he stopped shouting. I heard him go up and over the barrier a few cars down.

Go away.

Kit, come home. His voice was a hot wobble. *Kit.*

Did I want to live with M and Leo in Charlie's hotel? Did I think I could move in with Andrew, a person who could draw a bird's wing in detail but who was still a child living with his own mother? I just wanted to pause. To close my eyes. I wondered if this was what M had fled in the end, not his physical grip but the grasping in his voice.

Instead I said, *It's your fault that she's gone.*

It was mine too, I knew. Perhaps all he needed was to go to church again, to find someone who could talk to him about that huge animal God. Who would hold his hand and pray. Who could have summoned him his own miracle. Or not. Or maybe he needed some form of emotional management. Some trick of breathing or counting. I don't know.

He found me. He was crying. I hope you never see your father cry. Or your mother for that matter. It feels wrong. I kept still, hoping it would stop. I watched him come towards me, his feet quiet now against the grass. I could feel myself breathing. When he reached me he leant towards me. I stood, pushing myself up against the damp ground.

Could you be a normal dad? Would that be too much to ask? My voice was harsher than I meant it to be.

He reached for me. I saw the familiar drape of his arms, opening, enfolding. He put his head on top of my head. The brass buttons on his jacket shoved themselves against my chest. He wasn't trying to hurt me. He just held me. I smelt the beer, whisky and laundry smell. I let him put his hand against my hair and stroke it. For a moment, I felt completely safe. Like he had built his body into a wall around me.

There is a word for being entombed in a wall – immured. I learnt it when we read Poe. Our teacher told us that in ancient civilisations they masoned virgins who weren't actually virginal into walls to die. Those girls must have pushed at the walls, right? They must have tried to beat their way out. Probably until their fists were scraped raw. I was nothing like them, and F was not made of brick or stone, but something shifted and the air between my face and his chest grew thick and cloying. I could feel myself being held there for years, trapped in his arms and his smell, his denim being pressed against my mouth until I couldn't taste anything else.

It might have been different if my brain had been allowed to rest, to play in dreams, to take a single night off. But it hadn't.

I pulled away. Or maybe I pushed away. I was a swimmer after all. And in swimming that's how you accelerate. You send the water away and you go forward. But if I did push, it wasn't hard, just enough to make space, just enough to let the air in.

He moved.

I hadn't realised the way in which he was leaning against me for support. We were still on the margin between car park fence and cliff-edge. Weeds curled around our shoes. The earth was gritty and sandy, not prone to slippage. It should have held us safe. But I told you before that the cliffs around here are uneven and someone else had been here before me, drinking silvered tins of something. And his eyes were not night eyes and he stepped and he stumbled and I heard the crunch of aluminium and the fall was not clean. His tumble could perhaps be modelled by physics. The ways his arms tapped like xylophone mallets against the rocks. The way his shirt came loose from his trousers as it was kissed by lips of rock. But for me there was only my father and then a few seconds later my father much further down.

He landed far from the stage lights. But they were enough that I could see him. He lay in a question mark – curved torso and straight legs.

He did not move. And I did not move. Not in spirit and not in body. I stood, looking down. Above me the stars added their scatter-dash light, not bright enough to tell me if his palms were open or closed. If his eyelids fluttered or didn't. If his eyes opened to look for me. Then the shapes of the crowd came towards him, from all directions, like gulls landing on an abandoned chip packet. Soon he was surrounded by the bodies of strangers.

Over

I want to say that I ran down to him. I can imagine doing it –

The way my feet would have thumped down those steps. The way my hair would have flapped. The harshness of salt in my throat. The feel of his hand in mine. The way men in fluorescent jackets would have pushed me aside. But I didn't.

I looked again at the shape of him.

The boat game was over, and I had saved no one.

I walked back to our house, to my bed. I've consulted a list of adjectives to tell you how I felt then. Each word was too simple, too archaic or too fanciful. I can only tell you what my body did. I lay on top of the sheets. I held the pillow to my chest. My hands pushed into the centre and made fists there. I bit into it. I let the cotton sit on my tongue, the thin fibres absorbing my spit, my mouth going numb. At some point in the night, I slept.

I dreamt.

Or at least, I think it was a dream.

I felt myself lifted out of my body.

I spun upwards.

Tiny pockets of dew caught on the roof.

Up.

I could see our house. The kitchen's amber window.

Up.

I could see the sea and the bite-mark moon.

Dots of gold near where he had been.

The way the sea near the land was grey, catching the town's electric glow.

Higher and higher.

Lifted like dandelion seed in the wind.

Up.

Until what was below me was not sea and sand but darkness spotted by gold light like flea bites over the world's back.

I could not see F's body.

I had no hands.

No feet.

No legs.

I was nothing.

I was not exactly happy but I think there was a kind of peace. Everything was done. Finished.

I want to stop there. In the dark. High, high up.

But is anything ever really done?

He was alive but there was severe bruising internal and external, a dislocated shoulder and a rib that had broken and splintered into his lung. They called M to the hospital, she was his next of kin. He told her that he had slipped while we were talking. Charlie went to our house and bundled me into his car. It smelt of old coffee.

They had to give F walking therapy, breathing therapy. M decided that I needed therapy of the more usual kind. *To help you process.* My therapist was one of M's friends from school. I wasn't sure about the ethics of this, but I think he was cheap. He was a nice man, head bald and smooth as pebble. He gave me printouts with flow-charts. I did not tell him anything that mattered.

At first, M would not let me see F. She would not let me leave the small flat that Charlie had found her. The curtains in that flat were thin and red and they gave off a meaty glow. My room had spiders that were the same grey-white as the walls.

I slept a lot. Sometimes, I dreamt. Dreams that I believed completely in their unfolding but from which I woke up certain of their fantasy. I was grateful for these

235

nights, for their strangeness, for the way in which they dissolved me entirely. I was no one in these dreams, or everyone. I was the eyes in the ceiling. Then I was my teacher, then a dog. And then nothing. A tumbling haze of sleep.

Andrew texted, *You okay?*

Mm.

Can we meet up?

No.

Why?

I didn't reply. I wanted to but I didn't know what to begin to say. It was the start of many years of not knowing what to say. There were other messages which I let hang. Ghosting isn't nice. But those were spectral days. I hope he's happy now and loved.

I spent my hours watching daytime TV, grateful for the way that some broadcaster had made all my viewing decisions. I thought about F and what if the rib had gone a little further, had plunged a little deeper. I imagined what I would say to him when I saw him again. *I'm sorry. My therapist says . . . I'm sorry.*

Eventually, M said I could see him. He was still under observation in a shared ward. Someone had put a plastic chair next to his bed and I wondered who else had sat in it.

Hi, I began.

They say I'll be out of here soon. F's bed was angled so he was semi-upright. Someone had brought him a school-edition of *The Tempest* and it sat on the table next to him with a glass of water. His stubble had grown out into a short beard. He still looked exactly himself. Why this shocked me, I wasn't sure.

That's good, I said and then after a breath, *I looked it up. Camillus de Lellis is the patron saint of hospitals. He was a monk in the bubonic plague. Apparently, he was really scared of people being buried alive. So he made the monks wait fifteen minutes before burying the corpses.*

A whole fifteen minutes, F said.

I didn't mean . . . I had saved up this fact to fill the place that I didn't have words for.

I know, F said. *We have to sell the old place. But I was thinking of finding a flat. Maybe we could move somewhere new. Go to the mountains or the moors. What do you think, Caterpillar? Mountains? Moors? It's cheaper in empty places. We'll have a lot of room.*

Us on the mountains or the moors. I imagined the country coiled around us and the way F's singing would sound different without the whisper of the water.

I have to go to uni soon.

We talked a little about how I was thinking of applying to study Psychology. Not to be like M, *but it would be good . . . I'd like to understand people,* I said.

That's a hard thing. He patted my leg and asked if I was still with Andrew and I shook my head.

He said, *I don't want you to think that love is only like it was with me and your mother. It's not always like that. It's . . .* and he made a gesture, opening his hands as if holding something heavy – a bag of flour or a large plant pot.

You could have died, I said.

But I didn't. And he reached out an arm and I leant down and he placed the palm of his hand on the back of my head.

I can't live with you, I said into his shoulder.

Somewhere in the hospital a baby started crying. Somewhere else rubber sneakers squeaked against the floor. When F released me he asked if I wanted some of his yoghurt.

He died a year later. Problems with his lungs.

F never told anyone what had happened on the cliff. No police came to my door. No difficult questions were asked.

I waited to float off into the darkness of space. I didn't. Sometimes my mind detached from my body but I stayed on a short leash. Before I went to bed, I learnt to leave a show streaming with subtitles visible. I kept breathing. And sleeping. And walking. And studying. M calls me once a month and we have polite conversations. We still don't know what to say to each other. I did not tell anyone what happened. During the summer breaks at uni, I worked in the library, which involved much less vomit and sand than the museum had. I got a job, I was useful. I met people, fucked people, left people, was left. Did the things you are supposed to do.

Then I met you. You with your dark hair. You with that face that seems so transparent – every mood illuminated. That's what drew me to you at Alice's BBQ. Someone had tied a tarpaulin to the trees and we'd all huddled under it to wait out the rain. I looked up to see the puddle gathering above our head. Then there you were, talking to three guys I knew only remotely. It was so clear in the way you leant towards them, your face gently angled to the side in the posture of listening, that you wanted them to like you.

I don't think you realise how vulnerable that made you seem. I wouldn't have said it was love then, just a force, a force that kept me watching you and the more I watched the more I wanted to wrap myself around you.

I wasn't brave enough to get your contact details. That night I woke up, once again next to my own body, but for the first time I didn't want to stay home. If I'd known where you lived, I'd have run to you. I would have happily poured myself through cement to get to you. But the hours passed and I thought better of it. I told myself that you were already too open, too unsheltered from the world. I told myself that nothing I'd learnt at night had ever done me any good. I told myself that I would sit quiet and still. That I would move honestly and in daylight.

The first time you asked me to stay the night, I almost said yes. I wanted to be the sort of lover who woke up before you and popped out to get coffees and pastries. I wanted to stay in your bed that has two pillows, as if certain of the right to a companion. I asked myself, would it be such a big deal, if I split in your flat? If I spent the small hours watching your breath and reading the spines of your books, would you really mind? But I wanted a different kind of love. A less watchful one. I have never returned to your flat after midnight with or without my body. I have often wanted to. Sometimes I have wondered if we slept side by side whether I would always dream. Perhaps your peace would seep from your skin into mine. Maybe, I have told you all this for nothing. Maybe with you, I might be completely normal.

But for the first time in a long time, I want to be known. I can only hope that you aren't disgusted or scared. I am my father's daughter and my mother's too. For all these years, F and I have been conspirators. Only me and his spirit, wherever that is, know what happened. Complicit even after I left that town.

There were so many times when writing this that I thought if only . . . I have tried to tell myself I was young then. But it isn't that straightforward to separate past and present. I am still the same person. I'm still unsure when to hold on and when to run. But I am also a person who will do her best to never hurt you. There may be the mild scuffing that seems to be created when two people live side by side, but I hope we can have a kind future.

I've been looking for places we might rent together. I've thought, this is where our shoes will line up in the hall. This is the wall we will put our bed against. This is where we will hold each other until all the blood goes out of my arm. This is where we could wind together our lives.

Say yes?

Acknowledgements

Thank you to the friends who read early drafts of this book and to the friends whose conversations and encouragement anchored me during uncertain times of writing. In particular, Tony, Jacob, Abigail, Hannah, Kate, Ruth, Sharlene, Alice, Ellen, Jess and Eric.

Thank you to all the readers of *Harmless Like You* and *Starling Days*. I have not met you, but you made this third book possible.

Thank you to the team at Sceptre – Charlotte, Nico, Maria, Helen, Alyssa. Francine, thank you for taking me on in the first place. Thank you to the amazing C&W team – Kate, Matilda, César, Jake, Saida and Lucy, my brilliant agent.

Thank you to the MacDowell colony where I started thinking seriously about ghosts, which somehow twisted and evolved into this book.

Thank you to my family for everything. This includes you, too, Paul!

Thank you to the Whitstable Community Museum for answering a question about bus routes of yore. And thank you to all the coastal places that took me in as I drafted and scribbled. The town in this book is fictional but standing by the sea it felt almost real.

There is a teacherly saying that all books exist in a conversation. It is a cliché I agree with. I wrote this book over several years. I was influenced by reading that took place before and during that time – probably starting with the stop-motion animated children's version of *The Tempest* I watched in primary school. Or maybe it began earlier with every fairy-tale about a girl escaping home or a loved one twisting into a monster. There is not space to list that whole library. But it seemed fitting that I mention a few works of non-fiction that I looked to directly as I was thinking about the story I wanted to tell: *Daddy Issues* by Katherine Angel, *Insomnia* by Marina Benjamin, *Angels: A History* by Peter Stanford.

While the talk on out-of-body experiences in this book is fictional, it was based on one given by Nanci Trivellato. The festival at Stonehenge is a reference to something known as the Battle of the Beanfield. While Kit and Andrew only mention it briefly, it's an interesting moment in British history and in how we think about who has rights of access. Whether Jesus had sisters is much debated and it is not a topic on which I take a stance. But it is an idea that caught Kit's mind.

When I was writing this book, I wanted to allow for the complexities of love and rage that can exist within a family. Kit struggles to map her family situation onto others she's seen. I was not trying to write the typical situation because I don't think there is one. Violence can manifest in very different ways in different families alongside or absent of love and kindness. If you would like help and support negotiating violence in your home, there are organisations which exist to help those struggling with domestic abuse, and here are some of their hotlines: Women's Aid, 0808 2000 247; Men's Advice Line, 0808 801 0327; and Galop, 0800 999 5428. And I am grateful for the work they do.

Read an extract from

Starling Days

Shortlisted for the Costa Novel Award

'Beautifully written'
Spectator

'Exquisite'
Paris Review

'Poetic, hypnotic'
Stylist

Starling Days

ROWAN HISAYO BUCHANAN

'A quiet triumph . . . it illuminates both the difficulties and joys of being with others, but also those of being inside our own skins'
Sophie Mackintosh,
author of *Cursed Bread*

'Affecting and melancholy . . . Buchanan is a novelist of talent and grace'
Scotland on Sunday

'An exquisite rendering of love, sadness, and misunderstanding'
Paris Review

August

She wasn't expecting the bridge to shudder. It was too big for trembling. Cars hissed from New York to New Jersey over its wide back. That August had been hot, 96° Fahrenheit hot. Heat softened the dollar bills and clung to the quarters and dimes that passed from sticky hand to sticky hand.

It was night and the air had cooled but humidity still hung in a red fog in Mina's lungs. Wind galloped over the Hudson, pummelling the city with airy hooves. The bridge shifted, the pylons swayed, and Mina closed her eyes to better feel her bones judder. Even her teeth shook. The day's sweat shivered between her bare shoulder blades. The tank top felt too thin, and the down on her arms rose.

She took a step forward along the bridge. The tender spots between her big and index toes were sore from too many days in flip-flops. She took the sandals off. They swung from her fingers as she walked. Under her feet, the rough cement was warm. She wondered about the people driving their shadowy cars. Were they leaving over-air-conditioned offices, or bars cooled by the thwack of ceiling fans? Were they going home to empty condos, or daughters tucked under dinosaur quilts?

The bridge was decked out in blue lights, like a Christmas tree, like those monochrome ones shopping malls put up. Still, it was beautiful. Mina readied her phone to take a picture. She watched the granulated night appear onscreen. Perhaps her hands wobbled, because the photo was a blur. It was nothing she could send Oscar. But she wasn't sure it was a good idea to send him pictures. Not tonight.

She stopped in the middle of the bridge. Hello, Manhattan. Downriver, apartment blocks spiked upwards. She couldn't see Queens and the walk-up apartment building she'd grown up inside. Nor could she see the Park Slope apartment, in which Oscar was working late. He'd have a mug on his desk, the coffee gone cold hours ago. The photo of her would be propped up behind his computer. The sparkly stress ball she'd bought him years ago as a joke gift would rest at his wrist. Every hour or so he'd roll it between his palms. When he was working, he didn't notice time. She was sure he wouldn't yet be worried. She'd said she was meeting some friends after the tutoring gig. He didn't know she'd texted the group that she was feeling unwell and would miss movie night. He wouldn't expect her for at least two hours. No one was expecting her. She was unwitnessed. She lifted her face to the breeze.

The river was as dark as poured tarmac. They said that when a body fell onto water from this height, it was like hitting the sidewalk. Golden Gate had nets to stop jumpers. She imagined the feeling of a rope cutting into arms and legs. Your body would flop, like a fish. How long did they have to lie there before someone scooped them out? There was nothing like that here. People said that drowning was a good death, that the tiny alveoli of the lungs filled like a thousand water balloons.

She lifted one purple flip-flop and dropped it over the water. She didn't hear it hit. The shape simply vanished into the black shadow.

That was when the lights got brighter and the voice, male and certain, lobbed into her ears. 'Ma'am, step away from the rail.'

The police car's lights flashed blue and white and red. Once she'd had an ice-pop those colours and the sugary water had pooled behind her teeth.

'Ma'am, step away from the rail.'

'Good evening, Officer. Have I done something wrong?' Mina asked.

'Please get into the car,' he said. There were two of them. The other was younger and he was speaking into a radio. It was hard to make out his words over the wind and traffic. Was he talking about her?

'This is a public walkway,' Mina said. 'It was open. I haven't done anything wrong.'

'Ma'am, get into the car.'

'I don't want to get into the car. Look, I was just getting some air. I was thinking. I'll go home now.'

'Ma'am, don't make me come over there.'

Mina had never been in a police car. She'd read once that the back doors only open from the outside. Who knew what would happen if she got into the car?

The window was rolled down and the cop stuck his head out. There was a lump on his upper lip, a pimple perhaps.

'Where are your shoes?'

'It's hot out,' she said.

'Where are your shoes?'

'I don't want to tell you about my shoes,' she said. 'I haven't done anything wrong. I'm an American citizen.'

'Ma'am, where are your shoes?'

She lifted up the single flip-flop she had left. 'The other one broke,' she said.

Behind him, other cars continued into the night. Did they even notice her standing in the dark, a small woman with bare legs and feet? She was aware of the bluing bruise she'd caught banging her knee on the subway door. In the shower that morning, she'd skipped shaving her legs. In the beam of his headlamps, could he see hairs standing up in splinters?

'Ma'am, I really need you to get into the car. I can't leave you here. What if something happened to you?' In his voice, she heard the insinuation that normal women, innocent women, didn't walk alone on bridges at night.

'I'm fine,' she said.

Mina knew her stubby ponytail was frizzy. Bleaching black to Marilyn Monroe-blonde had taken four rounds of peroxide. Now it stood up in breaking strands. If she'd conditioned it, would this cop think she was sane? If she'd blow-dried it, would he have let her go home? And, of course, there were the tattoos twining up her arms.

'We can talk about it in the car,' he said. His shadowed friend was bent over the radio, lips to the black box.

Mina was tired. It was the heat, or perhaps the wind. So she got into the car. The seat was smooth. Someone must've chosen the fabric specially. This must be wipeable and disinfectable. People probably spat on this seat. They probably pissed on purpose and by mistake. Between the front and back seats was a grille. She would not be able to reach out to touch the curve of the cop's ear or straighten his blue collar. The flip-flop lay across her knees.

The cops wanted to know her name, address, phone number and Social Security. She gave them.

'We're taking you to Mount Sinai,' said the cop.

'I was just going for a walk, clearing my head. I don't need to be in a hospital. I was just clearing my head.'

Damn. Repeating yourself was a habit of the guilty. Mina tried to slow her breath.

'See it from my point of view,' he said. 'You're walking alone on the bridge at night. I can't let you out. I don't know what would happen.'

Only then did she understand that they must do this every night, drive back and forth across the bridge looking for people like her.

'I have to go to work tomorrow,' she said. 'My husband will want to know where I am. Please, please, just let me go to the subway.'

'We can't do that, ma'am.'

The car left the bridge and fell back into Manhattan. She kept telling them she wasn't trying to cause trouble. She said it so many times that the word 'trouble' began to sound like 'burble' or 'bubble'. Heat rose in her eyes. She pushed the water off her face.

Finally, they agreed that she could call her husband, and they would go to the paramedics parked near the bridge. If the paramedics said she was okay, she could go home.

'Oscar,' she said. 'Oscar, I need you to come get me. They won't let me leave until you come get me.'

'Slow down,' he said. 'Where are you? What's going on?'

She tried to explain about the cops and how she'd been clearing her head and now they wanted to take her to the hospital. About how she needed him to be there.

The ambulance was parked under the highway. Was it, like the cops, always there? Always waiting for people like her? The cop got out of the car and opened her door. He didn't cuff her or even touch her. But her breath came double fast. The pearly pimple on his lip gleamed. He led her to the ambulance. The steps into the vehicle were constructed from a steel mesh. They hurt her feet. A hand reached out to help her. It was soft and firm and female. It was attached to a slim arm and a body in scrubs the colour of the swimming-pool where she'd made her first tentative laps as a pre-schooler. Mina smiled into the face and the face smiled back.

'Please take a seat,' the paramedic said, gesturing to the stretcher. A sheet was draped over the end, which made it look almost like a real bed. Mina sat on the edge.

'Can you wait here?' the paramedic asked. 'We're going to talk for a minute.'

Mina nodded, before she understood that *we* meant the cop. He stood on the sidewalk, his legs spread. For the first time, she saw his gun. It was no bigger than a bottle of Coca-Cola. Then the paramedic shut the door. That had to be a good sign. They trusted her to be alone. Her body was reflected as a peachy blur in the metal drawers. The sour light marked every pore, every scratch on her legs, the tiny specks of dirt under her toenails.

The paramedic returned with a clipboard. Mina noticed then how pretty she was and how neat her hair. The paramedic's lips were lipsticked a dark red. Mina had once owned a dress almost that colour—oxblood, the store called it.

'Nice lipstick,' Mina said.

'Thank you.' The paramedic smiled.

'I just want to go home.' Did that sound too desperate? Mina disliked the clipboard.

'We have to do a quick check-up,' the paramedic said. 'Can you give me your full name?'

'Mina,' she said, then paused. 'Umeda.' She'd only had her husband's name for six months and it still felt itchy. To most people, she suited the Japanese name. Mina was short, with a small, flat nose. People never guessed that her DNA came from heavy-bellied China, not Japan's skinny island chain. It was Oscar who puzzled people with his mixed-race face and English accent.

The clipboard was uninterested in the intricacies of naming. It wanted to know the same things as the police: name, phone number, Social Security and address. It was as if this one long number and these few lines could tell them all they needed to know. They would probably be the first things asked for when she was dead.

Mina gave detail after detail away to this stranger. She said, 'Can I ask your name?'

'Sunny,' said Sunny.

Sunny shone a light in Mina's left and right eyes. She asked Mina to stick her arm out and then wrapped a grey tube around it. Her touch was gentle as she sealed the Velcro. 'This is for blood pressure . . . Oh, that's a bit low.'

'Don't worry,' Mina said. 'It's always been low.'

'Mine too. It's common in women our age,' Sunny said, unwrapping the arm. Mina wanted to take Sunny's hand and feel the low pulse of the blood. She wanted to say thank you for not asking anything difficult.

'This won't hurt.' Sunny placed a plastic grip around her finger and took note of numbers on a machine without comment.

'So,' said Sunny, 'how have you been feeling? Emotionally?'

'I'm fine. I was just clearing my head.'

'Were you clearing it of anything in particular?'

Mina tried to see what the paramedic saw. What would Sunny make of Mina? This patient was an East Asian woman wearing a black tank top and black shorts. A woman with peonies tattooed up her arms to hide the fine trellis of scars from her teenage years. A woman who didn't bother blow-drying her hair. A woman who looked younger than she was. A woman in bare feet, who'd let her pedicure grow out so that only the tips of her toes were striped in gold. A woman with a single purple flip-flop. In Sunny's place, would Mina believe this woman?

A hard knock on the door.

'Oscar!' Mina said. There was her husband. He looked like a real adult. They would trust him. He had a linen shirt. 'That's my husband. They said my husband could pick me up.'

Sunny did not offer Oscar a hand into the ambulance. She asked him to wait outside. Once the door was shut, with Oscar on the other side, Sunny spoke: 'Mina, I need you to tell me how you've been feeling.'

'I've been feeling fine. I was just thinking.'

'What were you thinking about?'

'I can't remember now. Not with all of this.' Mina didn't know why she couldn't lie better. She wanted to lie. She wanted to say, I was thinking about my job or where we should go on vacation or the trash schedule. Her lips didn't know how to make anything about her life sound convincing. 'I just want to go home with my husband. They said I could go home with my husband.'

'And you're safe with him? He's never . . .' Sunny trailed off, and all the things Oscar had never done hung there.

'Oh, no, never. Not Oscar. I want to go home with him. My husband,' she said, 'he's here to pick me up.'

They'd been married for only six months, but they'd been together for a decade. The switch from boyfriend to husband felt strange. The word 'husband' sounded so stodgy, so like 'my attorney' or 'my Ford Focus hatchback'. Tonight, though, she loved it.

Oscar waited in the dark. There were portholes cut into the ambulance doors, but he couldn't see Mina. Earlier she'd been fine. She'd been reading aloud a review of some super-hero blockbuster. They'd made plans to have friends over that weekend. He'd felt like they were finally getting back into the swing of their lives. For six whole months she'd acted like nothing was wrong. Every time he'd asked, she'd said she was fine. 'Fine.' And now they were here.

Finally the door opened and the woman in scrubs stepped outside. She explained that they could not allow Mina to leave by herself. Her activity had been too concerning. But they could release her into his care. Did he think that she needed to be hospitalised? Had she been displaying signs of depression?

Oscar thought of their wedding night six months before.

He thought of how she'd swallowed two weeks' worth of wisdom-tooth painkillers. He thought of the first day of their married life and of her body in the hospital bed. The cot had been rimmed by white bars. They'd put her in a paper gown. Every time he visited her, she'd told him she wanted to go home. She'd told him it was a mistake. That she was fine. She hadn't meant to take all those pills. It was like when you bought a tub of ice cream and you only meant to have a scoop and somehow you found you'd reached the waxy bottom of the carton. She'd told him the only thing that made her want to die was the hospital and its stink of piss and disinfectant.

The paramedic was waiting, her head tilted accusatorially, seeming to say that he must have noticed something, must have seen something. Oscar said, 'I'll take her home. She's fine. Mina's distractible. She's an academic.' He tried to say *academic* as if wandering around bridges at night was part of the job description.

'You do understand you'd be taking full responsibility if anything happens?'

'Isn't that what I signed up for when I got married?'

The paramedic didn't laugh at the joke.

'So can I take her home?'

'After you sign the form.'

They caught a taxi mercifully quickly.

'Mina, what's going on?' Oscar asked.

She tapped the window. 'It's raining,' she said. And it was. As each drop hit, it brought with it a bubble of orange light.

'Mina, I'm serious.'

'Nothing. Nothing's going on.'

'I love you.' He said the words carefully and slowly, squeezing her hand.

'Love you too. But it was just a walk.'

'Mina, I'm your husband, not one of those people.' He waved a hand to indicate paramedics, police, psychologists—

all the people beginning with *p*. 'How long have I known you? Talk to me, Mina.'

'Stop saying my name.'

'Okay, but I know it's not nothing.'

'I was just going for a walk.' She slumped against the car door. Her face hit the glass.

'Mina,' he said, 'sorry. It's just . . .' He didn't want to shout at her, he didn't, but volume would feel good right now. 'You could've come home. We could've talked.' Oscar eyed the taxi driver. It was hard to see his face, though Oscar glimpsed a beard. It was impossible to tell if the man was listening. Surely he'd heard worse. This was New York, after all.

'You were working.' She closed her eyes, as if she knew how ridiculous the excuse was.

'How am I supposed to work when at any moment you could decide . . .' The things his wife might decide to do clamoured, too many to choose from. 'I love you, you can talk to me.'

She didn't reply and slumped further, rolling her shoulders. The rain ran ribbons of shadow on her face, and her eyes had a haze that implied she might be staring out of the window, or at the glass, or at a moving picture inside her head. He was reminded then that his wife was beautiful. Wild animals were beautiful in the same way. A sparrow or a fox carried an untranslatable energy in its eyes. She might've cracked that face against the Hudson River.

'Mina, look at me,' he said. Oscar moved his hand gradually, careful not to startle her. He clasped her chin. Gently, he swivelled her face towards him. He felt the hard bone of her jaw through her skin. 'Please, Mina, look at me.'

She frowned. Her eyes scrunched shut. The tank top had shifted, revealing the lace-lichen of her bra. Above that was a handbreadth of her smooth skin. It revealed nothing of her inner workings. Her eyes stayed closed against him. His phone buzzed but he ignored it. In the street a dog began to bark, and her eyes opened. It was impossible to see the pupils in the low light. His hand rested under her chin.

'Is this something to do with us?' he asked.

'Us?'

'Us, as in you and me, us.'

'Us,' she said slowly, like she was teaching herself English. 'No, not us. Nothing to do with you.' She gripped the hand that held her chin, forcing it away.

The cab stopped in traffic. Behind his wife's head, Oscar saw two pedestrians. They were kissing, their whole bodies pressing into each other. Both were so thin and shaggy-haired that their ages and gender were obscured. But the kiss was obvious. Oscar ran a thumb over the back of his wife's hand. 'Why, then?' he asked.

'I don't know.'

'You can't not know.'

'I was reading about that actor who jumped off and I just wanted to see it. The bridge, I mean.'

'You couldn't have used Google Earth?'

Mina shrugged. He let go of her hand.

Rain spat at the window. At some point, she began to drum out a beat, smacking the flip-flop against her lap.

Finally, she began to talk. She turned to the window and passing shadows stroked her flushed cheeks. 'I was at Alfie's this afternoon.'

'Which one is he again?' Oscar could never keep straight the kids Mina tutored to supplement the measly salary the university paid her as an adjunct lecturer.

'Sixteen, lives on the Upper West Side. Learning Latin because his mom thinks it'll help him stand out college-essay time. He's good at it too. Most of the kids don't want to be there. But Alfie just needs you to tell him he's doing it right. Chews his pencils until the wood shows through. Likes Roman history—loves all that pontificating about tactics, even though he's so skinny he'd probably fall over if you tossed a baseball at him.'

'Okay, I think I remember.'

'Well, anyway, Alfie, he's no trouble. And I'd given him this passage to translate. It's about geese. Basically, the story goes that the Romans are under attack by the Gauls. After several defeats they're trapped on the Capitoline Hill. They plan to wait the siege out. The walls are steep and they feel safe. There are kids in the Capitoline, women and slaves. This isn't a battleground, it's home.' Mina made a circle with her hands in the shape of a protective wall.

'Okay,' Oscar said. He stroked his wife's palm. Whenever she spoke about those long-dead Romans, it was as if she were telling a family story. She'd pause at the good bits, savouring them. But the Romans and the Gauls would not pull his wife out of the river. They would not have to identify her body.

'One of the Gauls finds a way to scale the walls. And by moonlight they climb. The Romans are asleep, lying on their hard pillows. Some are probably snoring and some are probably drinking, and others slipping out of lovers' beds. None of them are expecting the Gauls. But the Gauls are climbing.' Mina's voice was going faster now, having found a rhythm. 'The Gauls have daggers and hunger and rage. They want gold and wine. They move quietly and quickly up the walls. But a goose hears the strangers. It shrieks, and soon all the geese of the Capitoline are shrieking and beating their wings. The Romans gather their swords and save the Capitoline. This is why geese are sacred. They saved the city.'

Mina paused, staring into the window as if trying to read something written on the glass.

'That's nice,' Oscar said.

'It happened thousands of years ago,' Mina said.

'I know.'

'And they all died anyway. The Romans and the Gauls and the geese.'

Oscar pulled her against him, feeling the weight of her familiar body. The heat of her skin pressed against his shoulder. He pushed back an image of his wife cold in the river and said, 'Okay, so you got Alfie to translate this story.'

'Yeah, he did a pretty good job. And I think he liked it.'

'But?'

'But I just started crying. I don't know why. I kept thinking about how straw in the mud then probably didn't look that different from straw in the mud now. And about how geese have these hard pointed tongues, and about how it feels to scream. And also about how tired I was. Suddenly I was just tired right down to the knuckles in my toes. And the room was so hot, too hot. And I was thinking about the subway home and all the tired bodies. And I just started crying. I couldn't stop. I told Alfie it was allergies, but I don't think he believed me. And he's just a kid and his nibbled pencil was just lying on the desk. He's just a kid and he's already so worried.' Mina pressed the heels of her hands into her face.

Oscar touched her neck softly, stroking it up and down, up and down.

'What am I supposed to do? I can't be this person. I can't keep crying. What will I do when the new semester starts?'

'Keep crying?' he asked. 'You said you were doing okay.'

She shrugged and looked out of the window.

'We'll figure it out,' he said. 'We'll get the right dosage.'

'We're just going to keep upping and upping and upping the number of fucking pills?' She pressed the hands harder into her face, so hard it seemed like she was trying to push her eyeballs back into her head.

'Maybe you should take some time off teaching,' Oscar

said. He kept his voice steady. They'd figure out the finances. He'd do the maths when they got home.

'I can't do that,' she said.

'You can.'

'What would I even do? Lie in the apartment and feel sorry for myself? I'd just get underfoot.'

'Figure out that monograph proposal. Apply to conferences.'

'I can't go to a conference. Oscar, I burst into these stupid tears explaining to a kid that *strepitus* can mean confused noise, crash, clatter or din. There's no single correct answer. He had to choose.' Mina began to pinch the skin on her arm, until he stopped her by lifting that hand and taking it in his own. 'And I can't just quit. It's so fucking hard to get these stupid little adjunct jobs, while you hope that something more permanent will show up. You pray for the magic words— *tenure track*. I can't piss the university admin off.'

'Didn't you say Crista took six months' leave to have a baby? And she's fine.'

'She had a baby to show for it at the end.'

'Just say you have some health issues.' Oscar kept his voice calm. Mentally, he scanned their accounts. If Mina took time off, they should be fine. It would eat into their savings. But, he supposed, you saved for rainy days.

'I guess I was also thinking about all the nights before the battle. The people had to sleep knowing that the Gauls were outside. All that waiting for the situation to improve.'

The cab stopped. Oscar pressed a limp twenty and a crisper ten into the driver's hand. 'Keep the change.' Anyone who'd listened to this miserable conversation deserved a tip.

Mina stared at the door and he reached over her to snap it open. She got out, moving stiffly. She tilted her head up at their building as if this was the first time she'd seen it. 'I can't do this.' She made a gesture with her hands to indicate a *this* that encompassed their building, the street, the whole city. 'I just can't keep doing this.'

The flip-flop dangled from her hand. He snatched it. The foam sole was soft under his fingers, like flesh. The trash can was a few metres away and he overarmed it. The sandal landed neatly.

'We'll take a break. We'll get you out of the city. Just try to relax. Can you do that for me? Try to be happy?'